STUART'S TABLET MYSTERIES

THE CASE OF THE MYSTERIOUS GIFTS

Book 2

J LEDGER

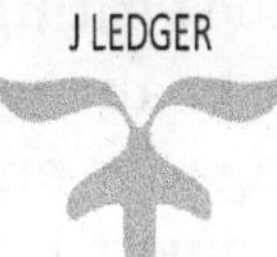

Author' Note: What Is An Investigation?

The investigative process is an evolution of activities or steps moving from evidence-gathering tasks to information analysis, to theory development and proof, to forming reasonable information that your evidence tells a story that is believable.

What Is The Main Purpose Of An Investigative Report?

The procedure of writing the investigation report can clear up your thinking and can uncover additional questions that provide new insight into a case. While writing an investigative report can be one of the most boring tasks an investigator may do, it is a very important part of the investigative procedure. As my mentor once told me, if you don't write it down, it never happened.

What Is A Scene Investigation?

An investigative scene is any location that will be related to a committed act which needs investigating. Investigative scenes contain physical proof that's relevant to any investigation.

Learning to be an investigator takes time and patience. Having the desire to find out the "Who, What, Where, and Why", that drives investigators to solve the mysteries which are always out there. I hope my book will inspire you to investigate the mysteries in your own life, and always learn to ask the question 'Why".

STUART'S TABLET MYSTERIES

THE CASE OF THE MYSTERIOUS GIFTS

"If it isn't written down...it never happened"

-ME

THE CASE OF THE MYSTERIOUS GIFTS

Book 2

My name is Stuart; well, that's my middle name anyway. My first name is Christian, but I like to go by Stuart. It's mainly because it sounds more professional and it keeps everyone from calling me Chris, or Chrissie, or even worse… Christie. I don't believe I have to worry about anyone calling me "Stu" until I am at least 40, I hope anyway. For now, I'm a super cool twelve-year-old detective genius. I may not be as big as I should be for my age, but I more than make up for any discrepancy of my size in the brain's department.

The house I live in looks almost identical to the other hundred or so in our neighborhood, typical for suburban houses. Also, my parents are not unique, special, or gifted in any way that I am aware of, so I believe I inherited my sleuthing abilities from my grandpa. My mom and dad are urban classic parents; they disappear in the mornings and show back up in the late evenings. They both have jobs and are rarely seen except for the weekends, but even then, I try to avoid them.

Don't get me wrong, I'm not trying to portray that my parents are subhuman worthless slugs on the DHR watch list, my parents are wonderful, as far as parenting is concerned. What I don't like is this, my parents are always asking me to stop what I am doing and get involved in their outdoor activities. But here's the thing, I'm not an outdoor type of person and their activities usually interfere with my detective cases anyway.

Then there is my grandma, who I call Nana, she stays with me and my family in our house whenever my grandpa is working out of the country which seems to be most of the time. I believe he's a secret agent and they aren't supposed to talk about it. Or maybe a world-class janitor sought after by oil moguls, I'm not sure. It seems every time I try to ask Nana about where or what grandpa is doing, she always gives the same answer; "Oh he's out working in one of those third world countries doing some cleanup for old uncle Sam. I've never met this uncle, but he must be a clean freak. Anyway, back to me. I don't want to sound like I am bragging, but I am a very famous detective. And just like other famous detectives such as Holmes and Watson, Wolfe and Goodwin, or Batman and Robin, I have my sidekick. But what separates me from the mundane, my sidekick isn't human or animal. It's a top-of-the-line smart tablet. Where I go, it goes, and as my sidekick, it helps me solve my cases. And best of all, I don't have to share the glory and fame.

Together with my trusty sidekick tablet, I solve extremely perilous cases and bring the culprits to justice. I investigate all suspicious activity and any criminal acts around my town and help the police put the bad guys behind bars.

Ok, maybe not anything too perilous or even all around my hometown. Remember, I am only twelve years old, but I have to say there is a lot of weird stuff that goes on in my neighborhood.

Mostly everyone living in our neighborhood believes it to be no different from anyone else's, but to a seasoned investigator like me, there is always something or someone worth investigating, especially in my neighborhood.

Just like today, it began just like any other normal day. I ate breakfast, got dressed for school, left out the back patio door, and headed to the back gate in a half-hearted attempt to make it in time for the school bus. But as soon as I opened the back gate to leave, I saw something out of the corner of my eye just sitting in the grass right next to our fence. Naturally, I had to investigate. My brain's detective gear began to race like a red-hot Lamborghini because now, there is a new mystery afoot and I am going to find out the who, what, when, and why.

CHAPTER 1

I Love How a New Case Smells in the Mornings

My school bus is never on time but this morning, unfortunately for me, it must have arrived before I even got outside. I've been waiting and watching for the bus now for at least fifteen minutes and no other kids have shown up, and of course, neither has the bus. So, since I am a detective and the only conclusive answer that I can come up with is the bus came early, or I left my house late. I sincerely doubt it's my fault though. Well great, the one and only time I need the school bus to not be on time, the sorry excuse for a bus driver decides to complicate my life even more by arriving early. Well, crap, crap, and crap. Nana is not going to be happy with me missing the bus again. But it's not my fault this time, the bus was just early.

Well, maybe the reason could be I spent too much time investigating the objects left at our back gate and I didn't see or hear the bus. Just like now, I am more interested in these mystery items than whether or not I may or may not have missed the bus. Well of course I missed the bus, duh! But this is a mystery that needs my immediate attention, and I cannot neglect my sworn detective duties.

Hmmm, I must have been seriously distracted not to notice the bus arriving. Come to think of it, I did hear a horn blow a couple of times and some kids screaming about something. Oh well, as Nana says, 'don't cry over milk under the bridge' or something like that.

Anyway, back to the mystery that has been laid at my feet, I mean on the grass, which technically is under my feet. I estimate that sometime after I arrived home from school yesterday evening and this morning before I walked out the gate, an unknown person left a very used and torn leather baseball glove along with a red sock on the grass in front of my gate.

I need my tablet to take a few pictures before the scene is disturbed. I am not accustomed to leaving evidence out in the open for it to be tampered with, but I will need to leave everything on the ground for now though since I don't have an assistant. It would be great to have someone to stand guard over the evidence so no one will disturb my scene. But unfortunately, I have no one to assist. *I wonder if I can talk management into adopting me someone I can have as a minion.*

Reluctantly, I leave the items on the ground to go back inside to my office. I will need a pair of rubber gloves, one extra-large clear plastic freezer bag, one small clear plastic freezer bag, and a paper bag.

I keep all these items in my file cabinet in my office. Of course, my filing cabinet, for now, is the bottom drawer of my dresser and my office is my bedroom, but that is only temporary. My mom, dad, and my Nana, who I refer to as 'Management', absolutely refuse to let me remodel my bedroom into an office, with a real desk and office chair, maybe a copy machine, and a filing cabinet.

Until my finances improve, I am using a small piece of plywood resting on two flowerpots for a desk. I also use a small beach chair instead of having a comfortable leather office chair. I use cardboard dividers inside my bottom dresser drawer to have a resemblance to a filing system.

One day when I am a rich and famous detective being interviewed on TV, this lack of support will be an embarrassment to them as I tell the world how I managed to solve case after case with only my brain and my smart tablet, a sock drawer for a file cabinet and a skinny piece of plywood for a desk.

I open the patio door and find myself face to belly with my Nana. "Why are you still at home Stuart?" Nana started as a scowl begins at her brow line then continues to the rest of her face. "Don't tell me you missed the bus again. How did you miss the bus? Or did they throw you off for another pepper spray incident?"

"No Nana, I didn't get thrown off, I got distracted and they drove off and left me. It's not even my fault this time."

"That's what you say every time." My Nana says as she stomps towards the coffee pot.

The pepper spray incident my Nana is talking about was not an incident, it was an accident. I have tried pointing that out to Nana, but she just closes her eyes while pinching the bridge of her nose and mumbles stuff.

This is what happened. The week before last, I attempted to make my own pepper spray self-defense device. Personally, I thought it was a brilliant idea but apparently, I am by myself in that theory.

I had the brilliant idea of combining a mixture of cayenne pepper, habanero pepper, and black pepper into a half-empty bottle of carbonated soda. I call it my 'doctored pepper', but I guess I could call it 'doctored soda' or maybe 'peppered soda'.

Anyway, I wanted to use my new "*DPD*", which is short for *doctored pepper device*, as an emergency self-defense weapon for my walks back home after school.

Just in case you are wondering, I do ride the bus from school every day with the hope that it will pass by somewhere close to my neighborhood and let me out within a close walking distance to my house. But that's not what happens, ever. The bus driver thinks it's hilarious to drop me off at any location other than somewhere close to my house. He says it's because he doesn't want me to have any trouble with the other kids in my neighborhood. I guess it doesn't matter to him that I stand next to the other kids every morning to get on the bus and he doesn't give me a predesignated location each day for morning pickups. I believe there is a serious flaw in his reasoning.

There's only one kid I have problems with within my neighborhood, well him and his cronies, so that's maybe three to four kids in my neighborhood.

Back to my "*DPD*", *doctored pepper device* story. The whole incident was an accident. It's not my fault this particular soda bottle had a faulty top.

My first day to carry my new "*DPD*", turned into a virtual reality nightmare experience in broad daylight. Right before stepping onto the school bus, I take the "*DPD*", from my backpack and bring the bottle up towards the sunlight to view the contents inside. With a squint of one eye, while staring at the sun through the soda bottle, I noticed all my pepper ingredients appeared to have settled at the bottom of the bottle. So, to ensure the peppers were mixed properly, I shook the contents up vigorously. Then I placed my "*DPD*", into the bottle holder of my backpack.

As always after getting onto the bus, I walked to the rear and began to remove my backpack to take my usual position under the last seat in the rear. As I removed my backpack from my shoulders, my "*DPD*", slipped from its holder and fell from my backpack to the floor. As the "*DPD*", hit the hard metal bus floor, the defective bottle top sprang off like a bullet from a gun, and the soda bottle, which was filled with the three different types of peppers, began spinning and spewing the peppered liquid everywhere and on everybody.

No one believes me when I say that hiding under the back seat of the school bus has its advantages, but today was definitely one of those times. When the mist and the spray finally settled down, I looked out from under my seat and saw that all the other students on the bus had their heads sticking out of the school bus windows gagging and coughing, the bus driver included. Eventfully, the school bus came to a stop on the side of the road and everyone on board made a mad dash off the school bus.

Neither the bus driver nor the students were allowed back on the bus and eventually, a tow truck came and carried the bus away. I heard it took several days to clean the pepper from the bus.

Charlie, the bus driver, refused to let me back on the replacement bus that was brought to the scene, so I was forced to walk back home, which fortunately was only a few hundred feet or so. But since my *"DPD"*, had gone off prematurely, I had to walk back home defenseless, except for my thumbtacks. And then Nana had to drive me to school.

Of course, I was sent to the school office to see Mr. Bibkins the school's principal as soon as I arrived at the school.

Mr. Bibkins wanted to know why I had a container of dangerous fluids on the bus. "Dangerous?" I said while using my perfected innocent face. "My soda wasn't dangerous; it was just my own homemade doctor pepper. It's not my fault the other kids, oh, and the bus driver, don't have a taste for the exotic." I had my arms extended out from my sides waving frantically as I continued to try and explain to Mr. Bibkins that what happened was totally an accident. I pointed out that it wasn't my fault the soda spilled everywhere, it was the soda company's fault for having placed a faulty cap on the bottle. Mr. Bibkins didn't seem to care.

There was no way I was going to confess to him my *"DPD"*, was actually a self-defense device, or he would probably escort me to his office every time I show up on school property for a mandatory bag and body search.

I thank all that's holy, after the incident of the *"DPD"*, I wasn't put in detention for the rest of the school year. Luckily for me, I had not broken any school rules or regulations. There were no rules prohibiting a student from bringing a bottle of soda onto a school bus, of course, there is now.

And as always, that new rule made me very popular, in a bad way. Nana had to drive me to school for a few days after that decree was put into place.

Enough of dwelling on the past, time to get back to the case at hand. Well only if I can stall my Nana for a few more minutes, I must collect the mystery items I discovered for further investigation.

"I need you to take me to school Nana if you don't mind of course."

I look at my Nana with my best sad face pasted on; I think I almost have a tear coming from my right eye. Hopefully, she won't be awake enough to see through my bad acting.

"Ok Stuart, give me five minutes to put some clothes on." Nana looked down inside the cup she was holding and said, "Make that ten minutes, I need more than one cup of coffee if I have to fight morning traffic taking you to school."

"Thanks, Nana," I said as I pass her by, heading down the hall to my office. I need to be as quick as humanly possible collecting the mystery items, Nana can be crazy punctual at times. I want to have both mystery items tagged and bagged before I have to leave for school.

I open the bottom drawer of my dresser, I mean file cabinet, and grab one large plastic freezer bag and one small freezer bag. I use the bottom drawer to store my office supplies and secret weapons. I also have a dedicated area in my third drawer next to my socks and underwear where I keep case files, past and pending, in that order.

I know my office supply stock is full because I made sure to check my inventory after I closed my last case where there had been pets mysteriously disappearing in my neighborhood and of course I totally cracked the case by discovering who was taking the animals and why…saving the day yet again.

And after my last case, I decided I needed to upgrade my detective bag to something more user-friendly. My old detective bag nearly beat me senseless while I was hanging onto the rear of a moving vehicle. I never want a repeat of what happened during the ride on the rear of the ice cream truck.

So, my new detective ensemble is a black tactical backpack with numerous compartments to organize all my detective gear. It even has a perfect size compartment for my tablet. I call it my 'tack-pack' because it's a tactical backpack. Sometimes people refer to their gear as tack, so my creative mind came up with the name tack-pack…that is such a cool name…I still get chills every time I say it out loud; "tack-pack, tack-pack, tack-pack". *Oh yeah…feel the chill bumps.*

I check to make sure there is a pair of latex gloves inside my tack-pack before I stash the two freezer bags and of course my smart tablet inside its compartment and hurry to the pantry to find a paper bag.

I no longer keep paper bags in my filing cabinet due to the amount of space the paper bags seem to take up. Even folded as tight as possible, the paper bags take up too much of the valuable storage area in my bottom drawer.

After a little digging through the box my mother uses to store paper bags, I find the perfect size and cram it inside my tack-pack with everything else. I am quickly running out of time, so I race out the back patio door and hurry to the rear gate of our fence. Force of habit has me stopping and peeking around the corner before exiting my fenced-in area to the world outside.

Everything appears quiet on our road, and no sign of a certain bully, so I make my way out through the gate. I quickly check my surroundings one last time before I retrieve my smart tablet from my tack-pack and begin photographing the items on the ground.

While I am taking pictures of the glove, I notice there are two letters written in black ink on the thumb of the glove. At this point, I am not sure if the letters are someone's initials or not, it is just the letters, 'TB'. Everyone knows if you write your initials you are supposed to put a period after each letter, these letters have no period. The letters could mean anything at this point. For example, "TB" could stand for "talking butterflies", or "twin beds", or even "two balls" …hmmm…might be the glove owner's baseball career highlight, "yay! I caught two balls".

I turn my attention to the sock that's lying next to the glove. The sock has no identifying markers that I can see immediately. It's just a plain red sock. There is a hole in the toe about where someone's long middle toe would protrude. I'm not a bloodhound so it won't do me any good to smell it, not that I even considered going there.

After the quick photo shoot, I take the rubber gloves from my tack-pack and put them on. I then take the paper bag from my pack, carefully unfold it, and place it on the ground. Next, I retrieve the small freezer bag from my tack-pack and after carefully picking the sock up, I place it inside the little freezer bag. I then close the zipper on the bag, sealing the freezer bag closed, taking my marker from my tack-pack, I write on the face of the freezer bag: 'ONE RED SOCK – FOUND ON NORTH LAWN BY GATE – 11/12 AT 0724 HOURS'.

I place the freezer bag with the newly acquired sock inside the paper bag and pull out the large freezer bag from my tack-pack. I get down on my hands and knees in front of the baseball glove and slowly lift one side to look under it.

I was hoping I would find a note underneath the glove…not sure what I was expecting the note to say…maybe something like; *"Hi Stuart, I thought you might like to take up baseball, so I left you an old used fielder's mitt and my worn and dirty lucky sock to wear around your neck."* But when I looked under the glove, there was nothing but grass…and a spider. Why did it have to be a spider? I hate spiders. Why couldn't it have been a small brown cricket, or a grasshopper, or even a lizard? It just had to be a hairy-legged creepy crawly spider under the glove. This of course puts an unforeseen hazard to this case, but as always, I am prepared for the unexpected.

Since I have experience in dealing with hazardous items, I always come prepared for any surprises. I reach inside my tack-pack and pull out a pair of grilling tongs. "Perfect," I say out loud.

I grab the handle of the tongs and reach down to pinch the thumb of the glove between the two ends of the tong that extend out. Holding the glove thumb as tight as I can, I slowly lift the glove up and away from the spider. And just to be on the safe side, I then toss the glove in the air, tongs and all, and let both hit the ground with a muffled thud. *There, that should take care of any spiders.*

I pick the baseball glove up from the ground with the tongs, giving it a cautious look for any creepier creepy crawlies, and then place the glove inside the large freezer bag. The baseball glove is almost too big for the freezer bag, but I manage to squeeze it inside, and just barely can slide the bag's plastic zipper closed. I quickly write on the front of the freezer bag the item's description and place it inside the paper bag with the sock.

With both items now secure inside the paper bag, I fold the top closed and scan my evidence scene. I reach down and pick up my grilling tongs and return them to my tack-pack, and then sling the pack over my shoulder. I grab the paper bag and make a mad dash to my office. As soon as I get inside my office, I place the bag on my desk and slide my tack-pack from my back. I dig around inside my tack-pack and retrieve my stapler. After folding the top of the paper bag twice, I quickly scribble today's date across the folded top.

Next, I write a list of the contents of the bag on the outside. A part of what makes me a great detective is being very meticulous with any evidence in the cases I work, plus I firmly believe in the old adage, 'If you don't write it down, it never happened.' Of course, I prefer to type everything using my tablet. But until someone in management buys me a label printer, I am stuck with writing the contents of evidence with a marker on paper bags.

My timing couldn't have been more perfect because as soon as I placed the bag beside my desk, Nana stuck her head inside the doorway of my room and told me she was ready to leave.

"To help you begin your investigative journey, an investigator's case log will be at the end of each chapter to assist you in your investigation."

INVESTIGATION LOG

DATE: _______________ TIME: _______________

LOCATION: ____

INCIDENT DETAILS: ____

____

____

____

____

____

____

WITNESS STATEMENT: ____

____

____

____

____

NAMES LIST

VICTIM: (1)____

         (2)____

WITNESS: (1)____

         (2)____

SUSPECT: (1)____

         (2)____

INVESTIGATION LOG

DATE: _______________ TIME: _______________

LOCATION: ____

INCIDENT DETAILS: ____

____

____

____

____

____

____

WITNESS STATEMENT: _______________________________________

____

____

____

____

NAMES LIST

VICTIM: (1)____

(2)____

WITNESS: (1)____

(2)____

SUSPECT: (1)____

(2)____

INVESTIGATION LOG

DATE: _______________ TIME: _______________

LOCATION: ____

INCIDENT DETAILS: ____

____

____

____

____

____

____

WITNESS STATEMENT: ______________________________________

____

____

____

____

NAMES LIST

VICTIM: (1)____

(2)____

WITNESS: (1)____

(2)____

SUSPECT: (1)____

(2)____

INVESTIGATION LOG

DATE: _______________ TIME: _______________

LOCATION: ____

INCIDENT DETAILS: ____

____

____

____

____

____

____

WITNESS STATEMENT: _______________________________________

____

____

____

____

NAMES LIST

VICTIM: (1)____

(2)____

WITNESS: (1)____

(2)____

SUSPECT: (1)____

(2)____

CHAPTER 2

Winter Wonder Land

At last, the bell rings and I reluctantly walk inside the room of my final class of the day, wishing...no...praying for the next school bell to hurry up and ring, announcing the end of yet another not so exciting day of Math, English, mashed potatoes with a lump of unknown brown meat, and then Science. And now last and of course least, an incredibly mind-numbing, brain squeezing, one whole hour of art class.

I'm so excited, oh boy and whoopee...art class, where I waste an hour of my precious life every day in school...painting or drawing something of nonimportance. I can never grasp the need for me to practice painting or drawing. If I want a picture of someone or something, I know how to do searches on the internet with my smart tablet. At the very least, I could just use my tablet and take a picture.

In art class today, our assignment is to paint a winter scene. I am assuming this '*winter scene*' is supposed to be a fictional painting. I have never seen it snow here, not in my twelve years of life. If I had my tablet, I could easily find a pleasant wintery scene and paint my rendition. But no…I can't have my tablet at school anymore, I might hack into the sprinkler system again, blah blah blah. Ugh… I will just have to use my extremely brilliant imagination on this one I suppose.

About midway through my exciting art class, the art teacher, Ms. Haylee, begins walking around the classroom admiring everyone's work. When she arrives at my desk, I hand her my painting and tell her I am finished and would like to read for the rest of the class time. *I have the newest copy of 'Gamer magazine' in my backpack.*

Ms. Haylee stares at my painting, flipping it over several times, and then she hands it back. "Stuart", she says, "I don't understand what this picture is supposed to be. The only thing you have painted here is a large black spot"

"It's my winter scene. Look at it again." I said as I hand the painting back. As she takes it from me, I point at the huge black spot I painted on the paper. "It's a snowman…well a close-up of snowman's face…that black area is his eye."

Ms. Haylee gives me a hard look and then wads my painting up. "You are going to have to do better than this Stuart." She says as she walks to the trash can and discards my work of art. I'm trying to ignore her, but then she walks back to the student sitting closest to me, giving me some sort of eye stare, surely, she doesn't think she can intimidate me, I've been given the stink eye by scarier people than her.

'I'm a detective, not an artist' I think to myself, then I proceed to pull out three more sheets of paper and I began painting large black spots on each piece, just like my first one. When I am through with each painting, I neatly place all three works of art in front of me onto my worktable. I walk over to the supply cabinet and retrieve a roll of clear tape. Using the clear tape, I join the first two paintings together side by side. Then I take the third painting and position it directly under the first two so that it sits directly below the other two black spots.

"There," I say out loud. With my artwork now finished, I carefully carry my paintings by the top two corners over to the hanging board. The hanging board is where students proudly display their new illustrations when finished. I pin my new creation on the board proudly.

"Ms. Haylee sees me as I pin my painting up and walks over to the board. She stares at my artwork for a few moments before eventually saying, "Ok Stuart, I give up…explain to me what it is you have painted this time?"

I look at her smiling, proud of my artwork, and say, "It's still a snowman's face, I have moved the view back enough to show both eyes and his nose."

Ms. Haylee rolls her eyes at me and takes her red marker from the pocket of her skirt. She leans over with a frown on her face and writes a large 'D' beside the black spot of the bottom painting.

I stare at my paintings for a few moments and then I walk over to my work area. I grab a clean paintbrush and a small tube of red paint and hurry back over to the hanging board. I take my paintbrush and squeeze a glob of red paint onto the end of it.

With my brush full of the red paint, I start filling in the large 'D' Ms. Haylee had just scribbled on my beautiful work of art, being careful not to go outside of her line. When I finish, I step back and admire the additional artwork on my paintings.

Now, my snowman's face just looks like he is sticking his tongue out. As I am standing there admiring what I believe to be my best work of art yet, Ms. Haylee comes to the hanging board and stares at my glorious creation. Next, she takes her red marker and writes a huge 'F' across all three paintings.

I stare at MS. Haylee blankly as she turns and walks away from the board without a word. Clearly, she is not much of an art critic, or she would see the genius in my rendition of a winter scene snowman. "Well, crap!" I say as I turn and walk back to my area.

The last bell finally rings and after a quick stop at my locker, I jump into the flow of students making their way to the exit. When I pass through the doorway, I stop momentarily and take a few deep breaths of air, and then some bozo pushes me from the back and says, "Quit blocking the door you little nerd, you're holding everyone up."

I grab my backpack from the ground which had fallen when I was shoved from the back, and make my way to the school bus, taking my usual place at the rear of the bus under the seat. I pull my 'Gamer' magazine out from my backpack and settle in for a long ride. I can't even begin to imagine where Charlie the bus driver will drop me off today; I just hope it's closer than yesterday.

INVESTIGATION LOG

DATE: _________________ TIME: _______________

LOCATION: ____

INCIDENT DETAILS: ____

____

____

____

____

____

____

WITNESS STATEMENT: ____

____

____

____

____

NAMES LIST

VICTIM: (1)____

(2)____

WITNESS: (1)____

(2)____

SUSPECT: (1)____

(2)____

STUART'S TABLET MYSTERIES

INVESTIGATION LOG

DATE: _______________ TIME: _______________

LOCATION: ____

INCIDENT DETAILS: _____________________________________

____

____

____

____

____

____

WITNESS STATEMENT: ____________________________________

____

____

____

____

NAMES LIST

VICTIM: (1)____

(2)____

WITNESS: (1)____

(2)____

SUSPECT: (1)____

(2)____

CHAPTER 3

Sometimes It's Hard Being Me

I exit the school bus and gather in my surroundings…hmmm… I know what I want for Christmas this year…a watch with a GPS. Charlie, the school bus driver, seems to have outdone himself this time. But yet again, I believe Charlie has underestimated me and my brilliant mind.

There are no street signs on the corner here where Charlie dropped me off, but I can see there are markers on the next block up. I start walking in the direction of the next corner, determined not to let Charlie win these 'Where in the World is Stuart Now' games he keeps playing.

The street signs become visible as I approach the corner, "19th Street and Main St". The question I have running through my mind now is, will the next block up from here be "18th Street" or is it or "Boxwood Dr". There is no "20th Street" so it has to be one or the other. I know that "Main Street" travels north to south. That would be an insightful tidbit of information if the sun was out on this gloomy winter's day.

Crap...I guess I will have to do this the hard way and walk one more block, just so I can see what the next street is. I keep walking towards the next corner, all the while thanking the city's founders for putting sidewalks on Main Street. I would hate to make this trek through knee-high weeds and water-filled ditches.

As I get close enough to read street signs at the next block, I see that it does in fact say, "Boxwood Drive". "Crap!" I mumble out loud and do an about-face and begin walking in the opposite direction of Boxwood Drive. At least I know where I am now and how to get home in the quickest route possible. It is times like these I am thankful for my detective skills and my dedication towards preparation, it certainly pays off. Of course, the city map I have in my backpack helps tremendously also.

I make it to the back gate entrance of my house only slightly later than I normally do, not enough to cause alarm from my Nana though. The cold and damp weather today has driven my Nana indoors. On any other day, Nana would be sitting outside in her favorite chair, oblivious to the world around her as she loses herself somewhere in social media land.

I open the patio door and find Nana sitting at the kitchen bar with a cup of coffee in one hand and her phone in the other. I grin to myself as I wonder what kind of frantic hissy fit she would throw if I hid her phone from her. *Nope, I value my life* too much to hide her phone.

"Hi, Nana," I say as I pass by her on my way to the kitchen pantry. There is a peanut butter fold-over in my immediate future and I don't want to start a conversation with Nana before I can make that happen.

I drop my backpack at the end of the bar and open the door to the pantry. Just as I step inside, I hear Nana say, "Hold it buster...if you are about to do what it is I think you are about to do...you better go wash your hands before you put your dirty little fingers all over the bread."

"Awe Nana, I was just getting the loaf of bread and peanut butter out first…I was going to wash my hands."

"Yeah…sure you were Sherlock…just like I was planning on making macaroni with cheese and corn dogs for dinner tonight," Nana tells me without looking up from her phone.

"Really Nana, macaroni, and cheese tonight! And corn dogs also! Wow, I can't believe you are finally going to cook two of my favorite foods," I say, bouncing up and down excitedly at the news. Nana looks up at me while setting her phone and coffee on the counter. "You really don't comprehend sarcasm, do you?" Nana shakes her head at me and says, "I will make you macaroni and cheese tonight, but no corn dogs."

"Huh? No corn dogs? Were you teasing me, Nana? You know I don't like to be teased, especially about macaroni and cheese, or corn dogs, and of course peanut butter."

I see Nana just shaking her head without looking up, so I hurry over to the sink to wash my hands. After making two peanut butter fold-over sandwiches, I grab a juice box from the refrigerator and head to my office.

I settle in at my desk and ponder over my new case as I eat my snack. It's been nearly ten hours since my discovery of the two mystery items this morning, a baseball glove, and a sock, and so far, no one has come to claim ownership. That would lead me to believe either the owner does not know the items are missing, or the items have been stolen and someone is trying to frame me for the crime.

I can eliminate the last theory; no one would be so crazy enough to try and frame a crime on a highly-skilled detective such as me. So that would mean somehow, the items were taken from the owner without their knowledge and then placed in my yard for some unknown reason.

Wow, this is a mystery. Ok then…it's time for me to do what I do best…serious case-solving detective work.

I take my smart tablet from its charger and power it on. While my tablet is booting up, I place the bag with the mystery items on top of my desk and begin pulling the staples from the fold in the top of the bag. I didn't bother taping the bag shut because I knew I would need to examine the items in further detail.

I pull each item from the paper bag and place them on my desk. I retrieve the baseball glove from its plastic bag and set the glove in front of me so I can get a closer look. I gather my flashlight and magnifying glass from my tack-pack and pull the baseball glove closer for examination. "Tack-pack". I say out loud. *Yeah, I like the sound of that word.*

I start at the thumb area of the glove and with my magnifying glass and flashlight; I begin a slow and painstaking inspection of the glove, pausing at even the tiniest markings on the worn leather of the glove.

I use my tablet to photograph each new marking or scratch I find, taking care to log the description of each abnormality, no matter how small. This glove has a story to tell, and I aim to find out what that story is.

As I make it to the large black letters 'TB' written on the outside thumb, I photograph the letters from several different angles, just in case there is a hidden meaning, like a cryptogram, but with only two letters.

The letter T and the letter B placed together as an abbreviation have numerous possibilities. The same goes for using the letters as initials for someone's name.

I pull the internet search engine up on my tablet and type the words; TB abbreviation in the search box. Almost immediately my tablet displays several sites that appear to be helpful.

I go through each site and begin listing all the words TB would be an acronym for. After filling up three pages of words that TB can stand for, I look at my list and blow out a heavy breath. I never would have imagined there would be this many words TB could be used for as an abbreviation. There is "to be", "too bad", "tuberculosis", "textbook", "text back", the list seemed to be growing by leaps and bounds. There are just so many different words for TB, without it being used in the context of something familiar, no one could ever guess the meaning of the two letters, TB.

I begin to feel like I am spinning my wheels and going nowhere so I stop everything I am doing and sit and think for a few moments. After about five minutes of zero percent brain activity, I get up from my chair and make my way back to the kitchen. There is nothing in this world that gets me motivated like a peanut butter fold-over.

A quick PBFO (that's code for peanut butter fold-over), along with a juice box and my brain is back on track. I suddenly have an idea to look at TB being initials for someone's name. This should be a little easier, especially if I limit the names to only people living in our neighborhood.

I pull up our neighborhood directory on my tablet and go immediately to the section of names that start with B.

I begin writing the names on a piece of paper beginning with the last name, or sir name, as some people like to say, and then the first names of everyone in each specific family. As I am writing the names of the 'Builder' family onto my log, I realize I also need to check the neighborhood names directory database for stepchildren and other kin having the initials TB. I like being thorough in my detective work.

I go through the registry of names, eliminating certain ones because I feel like they wouldn't meet the criteria for having this glove due to age or health. For instance, Mrs. Theresa Berring is an elderly woman that uses a cane to walk around the neighborhood. I don't believe this would be her glove.

After going over each name in the registry, I end up with four names that meet my scrutiny. But there is only one name on my list that my eyes are focused on. This one certain individual uses the initials TB, but he lives with his mother and his stepfather who have the last name of Smith. A chill runs through my entire body and beads of sweat begin to form on my forehead.

I have no proof at this very moment but my gut instinct and the goosebumps on my arms are telling me this baseball glove belongs to none other than, "Tommy Blackwell", I whisper out loud.

INVESTIGATION LOG

DATE: _________________ TIME: _________________

LOCATION: ____

INCIDENT DETAILS: ____

____

____

____

____

____

____

WITNESS STATEMENT: ____

____

____

____

____

NAMES LIST

VICTIM: (1)____

       (2)____

WITNESS: (1)____

       (2)____

SUSPECT: (1)____

       (2)____

CHAPTER 4

Some Dogs Are Corny

"Crapity crap, and double crap!" I say out loud as I close my eyes and lean back in my chair. How and why did Tommy Blackwell's baseball glove end up in my yard? Hmmm, maybe he planted it there so he can say I stole it and then clobber me. Regardless, if he finds it in my possession, he is going to clobber me anyway.

I need to find a way to get the glove back to him without it being traced back to me. I can't very well walk it back to his house, if he finds me on the way to his house with his baseball glove; he is going to clobber me.

I can't mail it to him; the Post Office won't ship it without a return address. And if I put my address on the box, Tommy Blackwell will clobber me. I can't hire anyone to throw it in his yard, because they would just rat me out to Tommy and then he would clobber me. Ok then, it's settled…I'm moving to Canada.

I begin to pace in the small space of my office between my bed and file cabinet. Not even a PBFO (*peanut butter fold-over*) can fix this. At this point, there is only one thing I can do. I grab my tablet and pull up my "Call of Duty" game. I need a brief distraction, and nothing distracts me more than killing a few online terrorists.

I am about thirty minutes into my game and about to set up an attack operation when my brain does what it does best, it gives me the most brilliant idea. I don't know why I didn't think of this before now, but there is only one way to get this glove back to Tommy's house without him ever knowing it was in my possession.

I have to do a secret night operation, a 'Black Op'. This is going to take some serious planning.

I put all the items back inside the paper bag and staple the top together. I will need total concentration so I can plan my nighttime blackout operation, so all distractions have to be taken care of. This means I need to get my homework completed before I even start planning my 'Black Op' strategy.

I grab my book bag and begin to drag out tonight's homework assignments. I go over the list and find that my English homework will probably take the most time to complete so I lay it to the side to save for last. I have to write sentences using this week's vocabulary words, plus I also promised my Nana I would work on my penmanship.

My teacher complained because she could not distinguish between my m's, n's, and r's... and that the other twenty-three letters of the alphabet appeared to be Egyptian hieroglyphics. I don't see the problem there. The Egyptians built pyramids using hieroglyphics; you don't see anyone marking their work with a big fat 'F'.

Two long hours later, my Nana pokes her head around the door to my room and tells me she changed her mind and made corn dogs after all, and that dinner is ready. Any other time I would have griped about having to stop to eat, but since we are having corndogs, I don't waste any time getting to the dinner table tonight. This is like a food vacation for me.

I grab a juice box from the refrigerator and sit down in front of two smoking hot corndogs. I close my eyes and take in a deep breath of freshly baked corndog air. *Man, oh man, these corndogs smell good.*

When I become a famous detective, I am going to make sure I have corndogs every night for dinner, maybe lunch also.

I finish my dinner and slowly make my way back to my office. I can't remember when the last time I ate as much as I did tonight. All I want to do is lie down and rub my stomach. I look at my unfinished homework still open on my desk and groan as I fall back on my bed. Everything will just have to wait until my stomach says it's ok to move. I close my eyes and try to concentrate on my Night Op plan and somewhere in the back of my mind, I hear my Nana calling my name.

I force one eye open and see my Nana in the doorway. "Stuart, wake up! I've been trying to wake you for a couple of minutes now. You need to get up and finish your homework, it's almost bedtime."

"BEDTIME!" I shout as I jump up from my bed. "Please tell me you are just kidding Nana, it can't be 9:00 already?"

"Close, it's about twenty-five minutes until 9:00, you've been crashed out in here since after dinner. If I had known corndogs could put you to sleep, I would have fed them to you when you were little." Nana says as she walks back down the hallway to the living room. I follow behind trying to shake the sleep from my brain.

"Nana, why didn't you wake me up earlier?" Nana turns around and gives me the one brow raised eye stare. "Never mind," I say and turn back towards my room.

I check the time on my tablet and discover I now have less than twenty-five minutes to finish my homework. I was halfway through with writing my sentences for my English homework when I had to stop for dinner. Hopefully, I can finish before bedtime; I don't want to have to rush to get dressed and finish in the morning.

I am just about to write my last sentence when I hear my Nana say from down the hall, "It's 9:00 Stuart." I know from experience not to whine about going to bed so early every night. So, I tell my Nana good night and quickly get dressed for bed. I am not sure why Nana didn't wake me up to get a shower before bedtime; it goes against her nature to let me go to bed at night without a squeaky-clean body. But I am not complaining.

I need to finish that last sentence before getting in the bed, so I turn my light out, so my Nana won't yell at me and go over to my desk. I grab my tablet from the corner of my bed and turn the flashlight app on to its dimmest setting. I prop the tablet up close to my notebook and begin to scribble out my last sentence for homework.

Since the holidays are getting close, this week's vocabulary words are holiday-related. The last word on my list is 'Yuletide'. I have no idea what this word means. I don't have time to look it up so I will just have to take my best guest. The word sounds like a name for a fancy dish you would order at a high-priced restaurant.

I quickly write out my last sentence; 'My family always eats freshly baked yuletide this time of year.' "Yep...that works for me," I say as I turn off my tablet and plug it up into the charger.

I pull back my covers and slide underneath, I'm not sleepy right now since I've had a good power nap. So I just close my eyes and start planning my Night Op again. The first step of this plan is to decide what time of the night I need to begin the operation. If I wait too late, our alarm system will be activated and for reasons beyond my comprehension, no one in this household will give me the disarming code.

If I try to go before dark, I will probably be seen and ultimately get clobbered. I will have to come up with a reason to be outside after dark... which's going to be tricky. I begin to go over different reasons for me to be outside and the next thing I know, I find myself walking down the sidewalk away from our house. I look around and it's nighttime and no one is outside but me. I look down and see that I have Tommy Blackwell's baseball glove fitted on my left hand like I was playing baseball. Then I hear the voice of doom yell at me from down the street, "HEY!!! STUART!!! WHAT ARE YOU DOING WITH MY BASEBALL GLOVE! I'M GOING TO CLOBBER YOU!" I hear Tommy Blackwell say, then I turn and try to run but my legs feel like they are made from spaghetti noodles. I hear Tommy's footsteps getting closer and he is laughing my name out loud; "Stuart, Stuart!" Then I feel him grab me and start shaking me.

"Augh!" I scream as I open my eyes and see Nana leaning over me. '

"You were hard asleep Stuart; I can't ever remember having to shake you that hard to get you awake. I guess we will have to put corndogs on the lunch menu instead of dinner from now on. Those dogs seemed to wipe you out." Nana says to me as she leaves my room.

"Crapity crap crap," I mumble out loud. *I am inclined to agree with my Nana about the corndogs. That was one messed up dream, and I don't ever want a repeat it.* I shiver once as goosebumps travel up my spine. I lay in bed for a few more minutes just staring at the ceiling. "Man, oh man, that felt real," I say softly to myself.

After going through my morning routine, I tell my Nana bye, grab my book bag, and head out the gate to catch the bus. Hopefully, this day will be uneventful, and I can get back to planning my Night Op this evening.

As I walk out the back gate, something catches my eye on the lawn next to our fence. I slowly turn and stare down at the items on the ground. "You have got to be kidding me…not again!" I say adding a large sigh at the end.

INVESTIGATION LOG

DATE: _________________ TIME: _______________

LOCATION: ____

INCIDENT DETAILS: ____

____

____

____

____

____

____

____

WITNESS STATEMENT: ____

____

____

____

____

____

NAMES LIST

VICTIM: (1)____

   (2)____

WITNESS: (1)____

   (2)____

SUSPECT: (1)____

   (2)____

CHAPTER 5

What Do You Say There...Partner!

I don't have much time before the school bus gets here. And I do not have any illusions that Nana would not be furious with me if I missed the school bus again today. Having no other options available to me at the moment without serious consequences, I set my school backpack on the ground and open the top zipper to pull out a pencil and a notebook.

Since I'm not allowed to bring my tack pack and smart tablet with me to school, and I definitely do not have the time to run back inside and retrieve it, I will have to do the next best thing.

I quickly mark on my notebook which way is North and South and then proceed to make a quick sketch of the items on the ground and their proximity to the fence. Then, using the eraser side of the pencil, I lean down and pick the first item up by sticking the pencil inside and leveraging it up. I bring the item up closer to my eyes and read the logo on the side. Hmmm, I do believe someone is going to miss these pair of shoes, they look practically new. I quickly toss the shoe inside the gate of our fence and then do the same with the other.

As soon as I close the gate to our fence, I see the school bus stopping at the corner. I grab my bag and run towards the corner screaming at the top of my lungs for the school bus to wait for me. I can see Charlie, the bus driver's face, in the reflection of the rearview mirror. I can also see he is laughing; in fact, everyone on the school bus is looking out the bus windows and laughing now.

I am almost within jumping distance to the school bus' door when Charlie begins to drive off. I don't want to be left behind today, so I run beside the bus banging my fist on the door's window screaming for Charlie to stop. I chase the bus for at least a block and a half. Finally, the bus comes to a stop and Charlie opens the bus door. "Well good morning, Stuart, would you like a ride to school?" Charlie says to me while still laughing under his breath. I also hear laughter erupt from inside the bus. Of course, I can't answer him at the moment because I am bent over out of breath. Instead, I just shake my head up and down at him and then slowly climb my way up the bus steps.

"Well don't take all day Stuart, hurry up and get on the bus. All the other kids on the bus would like to get to school on time and you are making everyone late!" I breathe out a heavy whispered "I'm sorry" to Charlie as I pass him by to go to the back of the bus.

Since I know the bus ride from my stop will take another thirty minutes or so before we arrive at school, I crawl up under the left rear bus seat and lay my head on my school backpack. I need to relax and slow my breathing down before I hyperventilate, plus, I need to ponder over the arrival of the mysterious tennis shoes left at our back gate.

So far, I have retrieved from our lawn; one red sock, a baseball glove, and a pair of sneakers. I am not sure at this but point, but I can take a wild guess and say that whoever is leaving me these presents must be some sort of sports fan, or they have a fantasy about me getting clobbered by Tommy Blackwell. I wonder if the tennis shoes are his also.

By the time the school bus arrives at our school, my breathing is back to normal, and my energy level has returned also. I'm sure I looked as if I was about to pass out when I got on the bus. I'm glad I didn't, that would not have helped my reputation as a top-notch detective.

The first half of my day at school went by at a snail's pace, or maybe even slower if that's possible.

During lunch, a kid about my same age but someone I don't recognize comes to my table and stands directly across from me. This new kid looks at me for a short moment and then sort of bows at me. Slightly taken off guard, I stare as the new kid proceeds to sit down in a seat across from mine and begins to eat her lunch.

I give the new kid a once over just as any detective would, observing she is left-handed, possibly of Asian descent, and apparently is fond of peanut butter and jelly sandwiches by the way she is downing the p b & j sandwich in her hands.

After she annihilates the peanut butter and jelly sandwich, she slurps the life out of a juice box and then carefully wipes her mouth and hands with a paper napkin.

When she is through with the napkin, she carefully folds it into a triangle and lays it beside her lunchbox. "Hi, my name is Niko." She says to me while holding out her left hand.

I stare at her hand for a few seconds and then release the juice box I am holding in my left hand. I quickly wipe my hand off on my pant leg, removing something sticky I must have acquired from my juice box. Then I grab her hand and give it two quick shakes before dropping it like a hot potato. "Stuart", I blurt out, "My name is Stuart."

After a few moments when neither one of us has said anything else, I go back to eating my lunch or at least try to. Niko keeps looking at me like she is waiting for something, which makes me uncomfortable which in turn makes me unable to eat my lunch. Not that I want to eat a ham and cheese sandwich anyway. Maybe just the cheese, but Nana said she was going to have me tested to make sure I eat the meat on my sandwiches. I don't want to go down that road. Just the phrase "test" was all I needed to convince me to suffer through a few bites of meat. Plus, I can use the protein to sustain me during my long walks from the mystery school bus drop-off points.

I place the remainder of my sandwich inside my lunchbox and look over at Niko. "So...What's up?" I ask her and almost immediately regret it. Niko starts rambling on how she and her family just moved here because her dad is some sort of scientist. His job transferred him here and that this was the fourth time she has had to move and start in a new school…blah, blah, blah.

I don't know what else she is saying because I started thinking about my new case and the new items that were left on the lawn and what it all could mean. Then I hear the word detective and I immediately tune back into her jibber jabber.

"Wait", I say. "What did you say about detective?"

"I said that I enjoy good mysteries and that I will probably make a good detective someday."

"Oh, then I guess you've heard of me then", I say with a proud grin on my face.

Niko looks at me with a puzzled expression and asks, "Why would I have heard of you, are you famous?"

I let out a short grunt and reach inside my backpack. Fumbling around only momentarily, I find what I was looking for and pull a beige-colored card with bright blue graphics dressing the front.

"My business card", I proudly say as I pass it to her.

STUART VANCOURT

"Detective Extraordinaire"

No Case Too Small-If it's Lost Give Me a Call

Niko stares at my business card for a few moments and then says, "This looks like you printed it yourself, not very professional."

It wasn't a question, but more of an accusation. "I did, but that doesn't make me any less of a detective. In fact, it is a testament to my good business sense, being frugal, and conserving resources."

"Hmmm." That was all she said in return, still looking at my business card. After a few uncomfortable moments, she asks me, "Perhaps I can read over a few of your cases you have solved in the past.

"I think I can arrange that," I replied, hoping this conversation had taken the train and was leaving town.

"Hmmm," is all she had to offer back again so I stuck my hand out for her to return my business card.

"I think I will keep this if you don't mind, I'm sure you have plenty more where this one came from." She said as the corners of her mouth tilted up slightly and she slipped the business card into her back pocket.

"Fine, I can always print more if needed." *I hope anyway, my resources are extremely limited...but I'm not telling her.* "My email address is on the back if you want to see my previous case history, just make an appointment." I reach down and grab my backpack and head toward the cafeteria exit.

As I stop to peek my head around the hallway before leaving the cafeteria, I see Niko in my peripheral vision about a half a step behind me. I turn my head and give her a cursory glance and then start my perilous journey to my next class.

I make a brief stop at my locker and exchange books for the second half of the 'Let's Torture Stuart' tour and then make my way to the science hall where I must endure seemingly endless lectures along with the dissecting of insects, frogs, and who knows what other roadkill specimens the teacher might show up with.

I glance behind me and on to see that Niko is trudging along still about a half step behind. I stop and turn to face her. "I have to warn you Niko, walking this close to me can sometimes be hazardous to your health."

"And why is that?" Her eyes give me and the surrounding area a quick glance.

"Over the years as a detective, I have made quite a few enemies," I say to her as I give my surroundings a quick look also.

Niko doesn't say anything for a few moments, only looks at me, and then she starts laughing out loud. "You are so funny Stuart; I would not have guessed you to have a sense of humor."

"I'm not joking Niko", I say as I turn and start walking towards my science class. "Ok…you've been warned, far be it from me to say I told you so."

Being distracted by Niko, I didn't see Tommy turn the corner and advance towards me. The next thing I feel is his elbow in my chest and me landing on my backpack.

"Quit blocking the hallway you little twerp!" Tommy says as he and his gang of degenerate misfits keep walking down the hall.

"Prime example number one," I say, still lying on my back.

Niko just stares at me and then looks back at Tommy and his gang. "I stand corrected; it is dangerous to hang around you. But that's ok; I can take care of myself."

"You say that now," I say as I make my way back to my feet. I start again for my science class, ignoring Niko and watching warily my surroundings this time.

I make my way into science class and notice Niko coming through the door behind me, but then taking a detour, walking up to the teacher's desk. She hands him a folded piece of paper and waits as he opens it, looks it over, takes out his pen, and then scribbles something on the paper before handing it back to Niko.

Niko takes the paper from the teacher, folds it in half, and then places it inside a pocket on the front of her backpack. Niko turns to face the classroom and then after spotting me at the back row of lab tables, Niko makes her way to the empty chair next to mine.

"I guess you will have to learn the hard way. I give it a week before you are running to stand in the *'I'm not friends with Stuart'* line. It's a very long line full of former friends and acquaintances. And I'm sure after a week or so of hanging out with the *'I'm not friends with Stuart'* crowd where no one is harassing or setting your hair on fire, you will appreciate the safety and peace of mind it provides."

"I'm not so easily scared away by grouchy bullies Stuart. I walk to the beat of my own drum." Niko says as she crosses her arms and looks over at me.

"Yeah, well you'll be walking to the beat of a drum alright...that drum will be your head."

I turn and face the teacher as he starts his hypnotic droning about...well I have no idea what he's talking about. I hope there isn't a pop quiz on whatever it is he is lecturing on, for some reason I find it physically impossible to keep my eyes open while the man talks. If I could just get him to email me his lecture I could have it memorized in a matter of minutes.

"Ouch!" I look down and see Niko pinching me on my leg.

"Wake up super sleuth! Class is over, I hope you can take mental notes in your sleep. The teacher said there would be a quiz on today's lecture tomorrow." Niko says to me as she slides her chair away from the lab table.

"Crap, crap...and again crap!" I grab my science book from off the lab table and stuff it in my backpack, then shake the fog out of my head. I have got to get it together. "This new case is I have been working on is very mysterious and has me distracted, and it has been plaguing my sleep also." I blurt out to Niko as a pitiful excuse, not wanting to admit that I was merely lulled to sleep by the teacher's never-ending monotone rendition of a science class.

"What's the new mystery you're working on Mr. Detective Extraordinaire?" Niko asks with a straight face though barely keeping the grin off her face.

I give Niko one of my trademarks sideways glances as we walk out of the science class together. "It's kind of hard to explain, I believe it would be better to show you all the evidence I have put together rather than to try and put it in layman's terms."

"Oh...I think I can keep up." Niko says, looking both ways before advancing into the hallway.

We walk for a few moments in silence while I quietly debate on whether to share my new case with Niko or not. Finally, I shift my backpack to my other shoulder and begin to explain what has transpired over the last few days.

I start at the beginning, leaving out nothing as I explain what has occurred and what actions I have taken as a detective. I pause as I wait to answer any of Niko's questions before having to dart into art class, thankfully there are none.

I am assuming Niko has art class with me because she follows me right into art class without even slowing down to double-check the room number. As soon as Niko was finished with the paper signing ritual with Ms. Haley, she makes her way over to the art table where I am sitting, looks the area over, and then takes a seat directly in front of me.

Niko quickly takes a college-lined notebook from her backpack and begins writing what appears to be a synopsis of our conversation, three pages of notes. Niko finally looks up from her writings and says, "It appears like you have been fairly thorough in your evidence gathering, but I would still prefer to go over your notes and take a second look at all the evidence gathered."

"Huh?" I stare at Niko incredulously, surely, she doesn't mean what I think she means.

INVESTIGATION LOG

DATE: _______________   TIME: _______________

LOCATION: ____

INCIDENT DETAILS: ____

____

____

____

____

____

____

WITNESS STATEMENT: _______________________________________

____

____

____

____

NAMES LIST

VICTIM: (1)____

(2)____

WITNESS: (1)____

(2)____

SUSPECT: (1)____

(2)____

CHAPTER 6

Best Bus Ride…Ever

Art class finally ended, and I begin to make my way to the back of the bus when I feel someone grab me by my arm. After a short burst of panic, I look over and realize it is Niko tugging on me.

"Sit with me." She said as she let my arm go.

"Hmmm…I don't know Niko, that's a good way to get you and myself beat up at the same time. I'll just go to my regular hiding place under the back seat." I turn to make my way to the rear of the bus when Niko grabs my arm again.

"Sit…it will be fine, trust me." She let go of my arm and I take a quick look behind me and see the older kids getting on the bus. "Trust me," Niko says again.

Although I am thinking I will regret it, I slink down into the seat beside her anyway, but next to the window away from the aisle. Inside I am cringing at the coming confrontation I know is coming. I leave my backpack pulled tight against my chest to ensure that it would absorb any punches, hoping they won't go for the nose.

As soon as Tommy Blackwell spots me sitting in a seat, he heads straight for me with a big malicious smile on his face.

Crapity crap crap…why did I sit here…I know better but I let her talk me into it. I hope she's got good health insurance. I hug my bag tighter.

"Well, well, well! What have we here? It appears the little nerd thinks he can sit where normal people sit. I guess it's time I taught you a lesson again you little worm." Tommy says as he reaches for my backpack.

No sooner than Tommy wraps his fist around my pack, ready to yank me and my backpack up from the seat, Niko grabs Tommy's wrist and twists it away from me. "Back off weirdo, we're trying to have a conversation." Niko blurts out at Tommy.

At first, Tommy looked shocked that someone would actually defy whatever he was doing. Then a look of humor crossed his face, and I knew we were both in big trouble.

"Oh my, it looks like nerd number one has found a friend. Tommy says as he turns his head back in our direction. I guess we will have to call you nerd number two." Tommy says as he looks around at the onlookers laughing out loud. "Number two…get it…ha ha ha… number two. I suppose you will have to learn the hard way just like your little friend here number two", Tommy says to Niko. "Nerds ride under the back seat of this bus."

With that, Tommy reaches for Niko and grabs the front of her jacket. Like something out of a "Jackie Chan" movie, Niko grabs Tommy's wrist with both hands and twists it in a way I didn't know was humanly possible. Apparently, Tommy's wrist agreed that it isn't supposed to bend that way because Tommy let out a scream that until now, I have only heard while watching horror movies.

What I witness next is even more astonishing. Niko gets to her feet, still holding Tommy's hand and wrist, and then gives Tommy a slight shove downward, towards the floor of the bus. To my amazement, Tommy goes prone on the floor of the bus. It is at that moment I hear the girly screaming turn into whimpering whiny noises…it's a really strange sound, especially hearing them come from Tommy's lips.

In a fluid motion that leaves me awe-struck, Niko continues downward on top of Tommy's back, his twisted arm going with her and hooked into the bend of her knee. Then she leans in close to Tommy's ear and whispers something I couldn't hear, but Tommy is shaking his head adamantly.

Niko then lets Tommy's arm go free and gracefully steps over his backside and sits down beside me. I just sit and stare at her for a moment before I look down and see Tommy getting to his feet. I really expect to be slapped in the back of my head, but Tommy gets to his knees first, and then without even looking around, makes his way to the back of the bus and sits down.

After what seems like a decade has passed and I can probably start shaving now, the bus finally leaves the school grounds and heads toward the highway leading home. I don't believe I have ever ridden a bus this quiet before, but no one on the bus is talking, not even a whisper. No one is even daring to look around. It is eerie actually and I am on the verge of freaking out. But far be it from me to break this moment of unholy silence. So, I sit and stare at the back of the head in front of me until we make the first turn into our neighborhood.

Without looking around, I lean over to Niko and whisper, "That was the coolest thing I have ever witnessed in my life. But you do know as soon as Tommy catches me by myself, he is going to beat me senseless."

Niko looked at me and shook her head. "No, he's not…trust me."

"Trust you? I've known you for only a few hours and already you've signed my death warrant. What's there to trust?"

"You are so funny Stuart, well this is my stop, I will email you later." Niko stands and begins to walk to the bus door.

"Wait up," I say to Niko, "I'm getting off here also. This is the closest to my house I believe I am ever going to get, and I am not staying on the bus with Tommy after you leave, that would be totally insane." I grab my backpack and follow Niko off the bus.

I am tempted to turn around and look at the silenced students who were somehow entranced by today's incident, but I manage to force myself not to look back as the bus pulls off. I decide not to take a chance at peeking over my shoulder either, afraid I would catch Tommy giving me the death stare, which will only be replayed in my mind as I try to go to sleep tonight.

I quickly catch up to Niko and we walk together in silence the short distance to her house. *Hmmm...so this is what it's like to get off the bus close to your house...I could get used to this.*

Niko stops at a corner and points across the street to a house that in all purposes resembles every other house on the street, aside from an exceptionally well-kept yard.

Niko's house is a light gray brick home with dark gray shutters and surrounded by perfectly pruned hedges like you would see on the cover of a "Better Homes and Garden" magazine. The sidewalk in front of her house is clean, and I don't mean just free of leaves and trash, her sidewalk looks like it was driven through a car wash. And the edges of the sidewalk and walkway to her door are cut clear of grass, grass that usually creeps its way across the concrete to join with the grass on the other side. Just like the grass, I see on her neighbor's sidewalk is doing.

Niko turns to me and pokes me lightly in the chest. "Do not say anything to my mother about the incident on the bus...Ok? She does not like me getting into confrontations."

"I understand completely," I answer back. "My parents always seem to think I am at fault whenever I am involved in an 'incident'," I say as I wiggle the first two fingers of my hands in the international 'quote' impression, "and sometimes on rare occasions, I am at fault, or in the wrong place at the wrong time," I admit. "But I have never done anything to Tommy to warrant him taking pleasure in terrorizing me...unless you count the time I hacked into the school's records and changed the grades on his report card. But as far as I know, he never found out that I am the one who changed his grades. And except for his Art class and Physical Education, his other grades were scraping the bottom anyway, so it wasn't much of a push."

"Oh, and there was the time I..." Niko puts her index finger to my lips and shakes her head at me. "Hey...I don't want to hear it... plausible deniability. I get it, you have a nemesis. Batman has the Joker, Superman has Lex Luther, and Spiderman has Dr. Octavius, you have Tommy and you deal with it the best you know how."

"Hey, you are mixing Marvel comics and D.C. comics in your metaphors...you are confusing me," I tell her while mockingly shaking my head.

"Ha, only a true nerd would have realized that...very good Padawan. There is hope for you yet."

"Now you're really messing me up by throwing in a 'Star Wars' reference. I am not a 'Phantom Menace' fan, well I am except for the 'Jar Jar Binks' character." I tell her, both of us grinning now.

"Oh, ex-squeeze me, mesa pretty okeeday," Niko says back with a giggle.

"Ok, back to serious. Let's go grab my bag and then we can go to your house and look over all the evidence." Niko turns and starts towards her front door. I follow her and keep any further comments to myself.

We approach the door and Niko pushes the buttons above her doorknob in a sequence and a green light flashes on the keypad and I hear a short beep. Niko opens the door and waves me inside as she smiles up at a security camera I am just noticing.

"Hey Niko, how was your first day at your new school?" I hear a female voice say from another room.

"Hey mom, the day went just as expected except for a friend that followed me home," Niko yells across the house to her mom.

"That's great dear...wait...what?" Niko's mom says as I hear footsteps coming in our direction.

A petite lady with dark hair which is mostly tied in a bun, steps around the corner of what I assume to be the hallway to the back of the house where the bedrooms would be. Niko's mom is splattered with paint and still has a paintbrush in her hand.

"Well, hello young man, and who might you be?" She says while grinning at Niko.

Before I can say anything, Niko blurts out, "This is Stuart mom, since we have most of our classes together, and for me to get caught up; we are going to work on our homework assignments together. And also, if you don't mind, since Stuart is more familiar with what makes the teachers happy at this school, we will be doing our homework at his house so we can use his computer. And it just so happens that Stuart's house is only a few houses down from ours."

"Well Stuart, it is so nice to meet you and I hope you will come back when you can stay longer. Niko, make sure you take your cell phone and be back home before dark please." Niko's mom says with a smile, giving us both a nod and a quick silent exchange with Niko before she turns on her heels and disappears back down the hallway she came from.

I just kind of stare at Niko unsure of what to say after that quick and extremely drama-free exchange between Niko and her mom. If I would have introduced a new friend at my house to either my mom or dad and then told them I was going to this new friend's house for a while, there would be an interrogation with hundreds of questions that would have lasted for hours. And if Nana got sucked into the interrogation, my new friend would, at the very least, be expected to present the interrogators with a resume with at least four good references.

And I am also curious about the little silent exchange Niko had with her mother. It was very quick and subtle, and if I had not been staring at the two of them anyway, I probably would have missed it.

"Do you want a quick snack before we head over to your house Stuart?" Niko says as she starts towards the open kitchen area. "We have pudding in the little cups or maybe a toaster pastry?"

"What is a toaster pastry?" I ask as I follow her through to the pantry.

"Seriously, Mr. Detective, you don't know what a toaster pastry is? It's a treat or snack you heat up in the toaster, you know…like a Pop-Tart." Niko tells me as she grabs a box of Pop-Tarts from a shelf.

"Why didn't you just say Pop-Tart, the way you said, 'toaster pastry', made it sound like something fancy. Everyone knows what a Pop-Tart is, and this is the South, we don't say *'toaster pastry'*. If it's sweet and you heat it up in the toaster, it's a Pop-Tart. It doesn't matter what the box says on the outside, it's a Pop-Tart. You can't be confusing people with words like 'toaster pastry' or you will end up having to defend yourself again.

Of course, I wouldn't mind watching you wad someone up and put them on the ground again, that was rather cool. And when I say, 'someone', I am referring to Tommy of course." I say while taking a 'Pop Tart' from Niko's hand.

"Not so loud, I don't want to have to explain my fighting on the very first day of school. And besides, it's not cool that I had to do that to Tommy, it's only cool that I know how." Niko says as she takes the 'Pop Tart' back out of my hand. "I have to put them in the toaster silly, that's why they are called 'toaster pastries' you know." We both bust out with a laugh and then quickly cover our mouths to suppress the laughter. Niko retrieves the toaster from the pantry and after opening the thin plastic wrapper, inserts them into the toaster.

The smell from the toaster has my mouth watering as I patiently wait for the familiar sound of a toaster giving up its bounty. Niko quickly makes two glasses of chocolate milk and sets them on the counter beside the toaster just as it pops up.

"Wow Niko, best snack ever." I tell her as I chomp another hot gooey berry bite from my 'Pop Tart' and quickly cool the heat with a large swallow from my chocolate milk.

"Do you normally eat a snack when you get home from school or are breaking you out of your 'norm'?" Niko asks me just as she dunks part of her 'Pop Tart' in her chocolate milk.

"Of course I do, but it's normally a peanut butter fold-over and a juice pack."

"A peanut butter what?"

"You know…a peanut butter fold-over. It's where you take one slice of bread, then spread peanut butter all over one side, and then fold it over…*voila*, peanut butter fold-over."

"Ha, you made fun of me saying 'toaster pastry' and you call half of a peanut butter sandwich a peanut butter fold-over? If anyone is going to get beat up it's you," Niko tells me while laughing.

"I usually do," I say with my head down, all humor from the conversation gone now.

"Not to worry, we're going to work on that also," Niko says without a trace of humor in her voice. "Trust me."

We finish our snack wordlessly and I follow her out the front door.

"Which way is to your house Mr. Detective Extraordinaire?"

I smile back at Niko and say, "It's to the right, just a short distance."

After a couple of minutes, Niko asks me, "Are your parents home this time of day, or are they at work?"

"They are both at work, but my Nana is there. She is my grandmother; she stays with us a lot because my grandfather works out of the country."

"Really, your grandfather works out of the country. Where is he working now? We may have lived there." Niko asks me excitedly.

"I don't know where he is working, my grandfather never says anything about where he is or what he is doing, and whenever anyone asks, he just says "It wouldn't do them any good to know."

"I don't even know what that means", I answer back.

"Hmmm, that is extremely curious." Niko exclaims and then asks me, "What does your Nana like to do?"

I look at Niko from the corner of my eyes just to check if she is being serious or not, and apparently, she is…well crap. "Well, this is kind of embarrassing, but all I ever see my Nana do is play on her phone. Don't get me wrong, I have a smart tablet and it has been a great companion and a great help with my cases but even I don't spend every waking hour staring at my screen."

"So, she likes playing games on her phone or what?"

"I am not sure what takes up most of her time, to be honest, I've seen her play a game for hours on end, but I have also seen her sifting around on different social media sites at all hours of the day and night. It's kind of creepy if you ask me."

"Hmmm," Niko says as we continue to walk. After a long moment of silence, Niko asks me, "Seriously dude, is your house in this county, or is it across the state line?"

"Haha, don't be silly, actually it's the second brick house just pass this next corner," I tell her while pointing at my house.

"Thanks to all that is holy, I was starting to believe you didn't live here. Where does the school bus normally let you out at?"

"Well…" I start, "that is a story for another time when you can stay longer."

"Huh?" Niko questions me while holding a puzzled look on her face.

"Look, that's not an easy question to answer without elaborating into the why, so… by not explaining the why, I can't answer the where?"

Niko just stares at me with her mouth open, then finally says, "You know, you are one hard to understand dude."

"Gee, I've never heard that before!"

INVESTIGATION LOG

DATE: _________________ TIME: _______________

LOCATION: ____

INCIDENT DETAILS: ____

____

____

____

____

____

____

WITNESS STATEMENT: ____

____

____

____

____

NAMES LIST

VICTIM: (1)____

       (2)____

WITNESS: (1)____

       (2)____

SUSPECT: (1)____

       (2)____

CHAPTER 7

Two Heads Are Better Than No Head at All

Niko and I walk around to the side gate entrance, and I let her pass through before me. We both stop and stare at the shoes I had thrown inside earlier this morning.

I squat down in front of the shoes and start, "This is the latest evidence that was left on the lawn this morning. Normally I would have bagged and tagged the evidence on the scene, but I had to put them inside the gate so I could run and catch the bus. I know that goes against all protocol, but I couldn't afford to miss the bus this morning."

"Well, at least your backyard is semi-secure. The shoes would have probably been taken by someone had they been left outside the gate."

"I had the same thoughts," I say as I stand up and begin walking towards the back patio door. "Let go to my office and gather some evidence bags and get started."

In my excitement about the shoes, I forget to warn Niko of the possible third-degree interrogation from my Nana as we walk inside. I am bracing for impact as I spot Nana sitting in the recliner with her phone in her hand.

"Hey Nana, I'm home, and this is my friend Niko from school. We have some schoolwork and stuff to do and I've already had a snack, so we are going to get right to it." I tell her as we are turning to go into the hallway.

"Ok, sweetie," Nana says without looking up. I put on a full break stop and turn to look at Nana. Something about her expression is off from her normal look. I am not sure what's going on, but I can tell something is bothering her. I know from experience not to pry; she will tell me if she wants me to know. So, I just turn back to the hallway and lead Niko to my room.

"Your grandma seems distracted. She must really be into her phone." Niko says as I gather some bags and gloves from my bottom drawer.

"Not that much," I admit. "She has her 'lost moments' with her phone, but I can see in her face that something is bothering her. There is no sense in asking her though, she is usually very tight-lipped when it comes to her private life. I normally just wait her out and she eventually tells me what is going on, well at least as much as she thinks I should know anyway."

"Anyway, back to the mystery at hand," I tell her as I shake my plastic bags in her face.

We both turn and walk out of my office and again pass my Nana who seems to be engrossed with her phone today. I rarely leave the house without my Nana asking me where I am going. Niko and I walk out from the patio door and approach the shoes without any words passing between us and we both go down on all fours at the same time as we come close to the shoes.

Niko is staring at the inside of one of the shoes and then looks up at me with a grin. "I found someone's initials written on the tongue of this shoe."

Please don't let those initials be TB, please, please, please. "The initials are 'TB'", Niko says. "Are those initials familiar to you?"

I answer her back in the calmest voice I can muster, "Yes, I do believe I am familiar with someone with those initials." *Crap, crap, crap...why, why, why?*

"Ok then," I say to Niko, "Let's get these items bagged up, and then let's go back to my office. I will go over the other items of evidence with you and of course, clue you in on whom I believe those initials belong to."

I open the first plastic bag and let Niko drop a shoe into it. I seal the bag and scribble the date and other important information about the evidence and the case on the front of the bag and then we do the same to the other shoe.

"Make yourself comfortable and I will gather all that I have on this case and then let you ramble through it while I look on the internet for any airline flights to South America leaving sometime tonight."

"You know, as I said before, you are one strange dude. And by the way, I don't ramble. I study intensely, or even sometimes sift through quickly, but never do I ramble."

I lay all the evidence and the case file folder next to where she is sitting on the bed. "Do you want a juice box"?, I ask Niko. "I am going to grab me one, it helps me think," I say as I start for the door.

"Yes please, but first can you give me a notebook and a pencil. I would like to take down a few notes." Niko tells me without looking up.

I hand Niko a pencil and tablet and then start toward the kitchen. I pause as I see my Nana sitting on the couch just staring at her phone. I walk over to her and put my hand on her knee, and she looks over at me. "I'm just worried about your grandpa Stuart. It's been five days since I've heard from him. It's not like him to go so long without calling me."

"He's fine Nana, I'm sure he will call you when he can. He probably got tied up on some huge cleaning job over there, what does he call that country? He calls it a third country, right?", I ask Nana.

"Yeah, that's what I'm afraid of, and he calls it a third-world country," Nana says and goes back to staring at her phone.

I grab two juice boxes and start back towards my office. "Third-world, that sounds like a science fiction movie instead of a country", I mumble to myself.

By the time I make it back to my office, Niko has all the evidence spread over the top of my bed covers, staring at it with her arms crossed.

"Well," Niko starts, "it would appear to me that all the evidence is pointing to your nemesis, Tommy Blackwell being the owner of the items left in your yard. I guess we can put a checkmark on the 'who' now, the real question is why were the items left there at all? At least that is the question that has me pinned against the wall."

"Ha, I like that saying, where did you hear that from?" I ask, being curious.

"Yeah, me too. I picked it up from an old detective show, it was catchy, so I put it in my collection of cool things to say."

"Well, I suppose the next step would be to try to catch whoever is doing this in the act of making the drop-off. I am not sure how we can do that; my parents are not going to let me stake out the yard all night, especially on a school night. Do you have any ideas Niko?"

"Well, it just so happens I do. I am going to run home and pick up some equipment, I will be right back." Niko tells me as she hurries through the door into the hallway. Before I could ask her anything she was out the back door and gone.

I glimpse over at my Nana who is still staring at her phone, mentally trying to force it to ring I assume.
I go back to my office and gather up all the evidence that was left strewn all over my bed. I don't think I would ever admit it out loud, but I enjoy having someone to hash over a case with. I hope things work out where we can investigate more of my cases together. I'm not saying I want her to be my investigative partner, only that I wouldn't mind having another like-minded person I can bounce off ideas with.

True to her word, Niko ran back into my office without so much as a knock on the door or a quick "may I come in". She just busts up in my bedroom like she's been living here for years. *Hmmm, I would have done the same thing, of course, it's just being smart and saving precious time.*

"Ok Stuart, this here is a 'Game Camera'. Are you familiar with how they function?" Niko asks me as she is handing me a camouflaged device with a latch and hinges.

"I am familiar in name only; I have never held one before. I had put in a request to management for one, but it had been deleted from my budget, claiming it was a nonessential item. I tried to argue and barter my socks and underwear, but they claimed those were essential items. It was like reasoning with statues. How did you get your parents to buy you one?" I ask her, handing the camera back.

"They didn't, I bought it myself with the money I earn from

working. My parents don't believe in giving an allowance, but instead, pay me for doing chores and other tasks around the house. And they even give me a bonus now and again for doing work that is not required of me or written in our list of approved chores."

I know I am looking at Niko like she has two heads, but what she is telling me sounds too good to be true. I have never heard of parents paying their children for doing chores around the house. My parents just always want to know why I haven't made up my bed, or why haven't I taken out the trash, or why am I still wearing the same pants that I have had on for the last three days. This concept of paying for chores is going to be brought up at my next meeting with management.

"Are you ready?" Niko asks. I am not exactly sure what I am supposed to be ready for, so I just nod my head a little and see if that gets a prompt out of her. And just like that she starts out the door and says, "Alright then, let's go find a good hiding place for this game cam."

Niko and I wander around the gate area of the fence looking for the perfect place to mount the camera so we can get the best photos possible. After a few nonproductive attempts, we finally agree on a location.

We strap and secure the camera to the rear of my parent's mailbox post, facing the camera directly beside the gate where the other items have been dropped off. Niko does a few test pictures and then adjusts the perimeters and timers on the camera.

"Hey, is the camera going to be able to take photos at night? It gets rather dark on this side of the house since there are no streetlights close?" I ask, wondering if the suspect does his drop-off in the middle of the night.

"Absolutely, this camera comes complete with infrared, capable of night photos clear up to 100 feet. With the camera only about 30 feet from where the suspect drops off, I believe we will have some very good shots of our culprit." Niko tells me assuredly.

"Well, all we can do now is wait until tomorrow morning, then we will see if we have any more items that have been dropped off. If we do, then we will have our culprit on camera. Ok, what time does your bus come in the morning?" Niko asks.

"Oh, hmmm, I believe it is 7:30 give or take about 5 to 10 minutes. Why?"

"Ok then, I will see you at 7:00 a.m. sharp. We need the extra time to download the camera and collect any new evidence. See you in the morning." And with that, she turns on her heels and trots off in the direction of her house.

Me, I rush back inside the gate, not wanting to be caught outside my fence in case Tommy Blackwell is wandering the streets with his goon squad and me defenseless without my backup.

I go back inside the house, and I hear Nana humming to herself and cooking supper. "I am assuming grandpa called you while I was outside?" I ask her as I'm heading to the refrigerator. I grab myself a juice box and turn to face Nana. It is good to see a smile back on her face.

"Yes, he called me, he told me he had run into a little trouble, but all was fine and that he was coming home in a few days. Just between you and me Stuart, I am putting my foot down. He is not going anywhere outside of this country from now on unless it's on a cruise ship with me."

I head back to my office; I still have homework to do and probably need to prepare some evidence bags for tomorrow, just in case. I have the feeling it's going to be a very long night; the suspense is going to be nerve-racking.

INVESTIGATION LOG

DATE: _________________ TIME: _______________

LOCATION: ____

INCIDENT DETAILS: ____

____

____

____

____

____

____

WITNESS STATEMENT: ____

____

____

____

____

NAMES LIST

VICTIM: (1)____

         (2)____

WITNESS: (1)____

         (2)____

SUSPECT: (1)____

         (2)____

CHAPTER 8

What Big Ears You Have Grandpa!

I hear my Nana call my name to wake me, and not wasting any time, I jump out of bed and rush through my morning rituals so I can be outside right at 7.00 to meet Niko and check the camera. I don't know Niko that well, but all my instincts tell me she will be outside promptly at 7:00 sharp. I don't want her looking at the evidence captured on the camera without me, even though it is her camera. It's not that I believe she is incapable or that she lacks the ability to think like a seasoned investigator like me, well, I do think that last part, but this is my case and Niko is merely assisting, with her camera.

I finish eating my cereal in record time and don't even bother to drink the chocolate milk left behind by the cocoa-flavored rice crunchies. I make a beeline for the patio door with five minutes to spare when I hear my Nana call my name.

"Stuart, you sure are leaving in a rush this morning, no goodbyes, no "I missed the bus", what's going on young man, something is going on with you so spill."

"Awe Nana, you're going to make me late meeting Niko this morning. I'll fill you in later. Can I go now?"

"Hmmm, so all it takes to get you out of the house early in the mornings is a cute little girl. I will have to remember that." Nana says while wiggling her eyebrows at me.

"Yuck Nana, that's disturbing," I yell back at her as I run out the door and close it quickly, not wanting any more of Nana's suggestions floating outside where anyone can hear, especially Niko.

I glance at my watch as I'm opening the back gate and see that it is 7:01. Crap, I'm late. I see Niko leaning against the fence and then see her glance at her watch.

"We will need to synchronize our watches, that way neither of us will have to wait on the other in the future", Niko says while giving my watch cursory glances. "Yea, ok." I simply say back. Then abruptly changing the subject, I state the obvious. "Well, I don't see any new items on the ground this morning, unless you've already bagged and tagged them."

"No, nothing new this morning so I doubt there will be anything on the camera, but for thoroughness, as any good investigator should, I will check the camera for any activity."

Niko and I walk over to where the camera is hidden in plain view, and I watch as Niko pulls the memory card from the camera and places it inside her phone. "This shouldn't take long, especially if there were no pictures taken last night," Niko says while working her phone screen with both hands.

"I was correct in my assumption; there is nothing on the memory card." Niko pulls the card from her phone and places it back inside the camera. "Since there is no evidence to collect this morning, we should make our way towards the bus stop and discuss our case and what our next move should be", Niko says as she turns and begins to walk up the street.

Did she just say "our case"; wow, you give a person an inch. I am still staring at her walking away when I realize she is not waiting on me. I hurry to catch up so I can explain that "I" am the detective and that this is "my" case. She needs to know that she is just a friend who I let look at my case files, and loaned me a camera, and saved me from getting clobbered by Tommy Blackwell.

Of course, that last part is debatable, if Niko hadn't asked me to sit beside her, then I would have been in my normal spot under the back seat, Tommy wouldn't have threatened me and the bus ride would have ended with me getting off at some unknown location in the middle of nowhere, like normal.

Now, because of Niko, I have to make sure whenever I am outside my house, I will need someone with me that can keep me from getting clobbered by Tommy Blackwell. And I know without a doubt he is already plotting my demise.

Before I work myself up into a panic, I need more information from Niko, so I can decide if I need to move out of the country or not.

"Niko, how long are you and your family planning on staying here?" I ask, remembering her saying how her family has moved around quite a bit.

Niko turns to me with a puzzled look on her face and asks, "That's kind of an out-of-the-blue and off-topic question, why do you want to know that right now?"

"Because my life flashes before my eyes when I think about walking outside my fence and running into Tommy Blackwell and unlike you, I can't pull a 'Jackie Chan' no matter how many times I've played 'Mortal Combat'."

Niko laughs and says, "You're so dramatic. Look, no worries. We're going to work on some techniques after school today but for now, let's focus on the case."

"Easy for you to say," I answer back. *Well, at least she did say 'the case' this time instead of 'our case'.* "Ok then, as I see it, we have four problems. We need to find out who is placing the items in my yard, why the unknown person is making the drop-offs in my yard, what to do about it when we discover who is leaving the items, and then lastly but most certainly the most important unanswered question, how do we get the items belonging to Tommy Blackwell back in his possession without him clobbering me?" I say to Niko quickly without taking a breath, but now take the time to breathe in a deep rush of air, which of course makes me dizzy.

"You seem to have a Tommy Blackwell phobia," Niko exclaims.

"No doubt." That was my only reply.

~~~

I am watching my art teacher desecrate my latest creation by drawing a giant red 'F' on my version of a starry night. Apparently in her world, stars are pointed and twinkle in the night sky. In my world, which in reality, they are round blazing suns millions of light-years away with the occasional 'black hole'. That is just what my 'starry night' artwork depicted, a beautiful black hole phenomenon. She said it was just a piece of paper painted black; I am starting to believe our art teacher has no imagination at all, maybe she should think about being a physical education instructor. I believe I will leave her a note with some constructional criticism and a suggestion of possibly changing careers. Maybe I could download some truck driving school informational flyers and give them to her.

As I begin to scribble out the note for my art teacher Ms. Haylee, the school bell rings, and I put all my belongings in my backpack and start to move towards the door. *Oh well, I will finish my note for Ms. Haylee later.* I pause momentarily as Niko comes up beside me quickly and leans over and whispers, "I believe I am seeing a pattern with you and the art teacher.

"What do you mean?" I ask.

"You paint something you believe is creative, which it is not, and then she plants a giant 'F' on the front."

"And?"

"Do you do what you do just to drive her insane or what?" Niko asks as she waves her hands around.

"I have no idea what you are talking about," I say as we pass through the doorway and head towards our lockers.

To my utmost surprise and total unbelief, Niko and I have an uneventful ride home on the bus. I follow Niko off the bus and turn in the direction of my house when I hear Niko say, "Hey, detective extraordinaire, I will be at your house in 30 minutes, wear some loose clothing."
~~~

"Sure", I answer back, "Just so you know, all my clothes are loose, my mom keeps telling me I am going to grow into them."

With that, she turns and disappears into her house, and I hurry down the street to my house, not wanting to take any chances.

As I enter through the patio door, I hear Nana talking and I recognize a familiar male voice joining the conversation. I drop my backpack at the door and hurry over to hug my grandpa. I can't remember how long it's been since I have seen him last.

"Hey Grandpa, when did you get here?" I ask as I pull back away from the hug.

"I haven't been home long 'little man'. Anything new with you, are you still playing detective, or are you battling alien monsters?" Grandpa asks as he gets up from the couch where he was sitting next to Nana.

I look grandpa over quickly; he still looks like he could take on a live bear in a wrestling match, but his eyes look tired. "I'm glad you're home grandpa, how long are you here for?" I ask as I head back towards my backpack.

"I'm not leaving home to work anymore; I'm retiring from my line of work. I'm getting too old to be chasing terrorists all over the world." Grandpa says as he walks over to the coffee pot.

"Chasing terrorist", I laugh out loud. "You're too funny grandpa."

"Do you want a cup of coffee Nana?" I hear him ask Nana, it's funny, he always calls her Nana too.

"What do you mean by 'chasing terrorist' grandpa; I thought you were a *cleaner*, or are you just making fun?" I ask grandpa as he makes his coffee. Nana has walked up beside him now and is grabbing a cup for herself. I tried coffee once; it tastes like drinking dirt, yuck, and ugh.

Grandpa makes a short little laugh and says, "It doesn't matter Stuart, what matters is that I am home and home to stay."

"Ok, again, I'm glad you're back grandpa," I say as I head toward my room.

As I go into my room and close my door, I quickly remove my school clothes and put on something that I guess would be loose, it's hard to determine that since all my clothes feel 'loose' to me.

I check the time and see that I have about 10 minutes before Niko shows up. I take this opportunity to dash into the pantry for bread and peanut butter. It is time for a fold-over.

After my snack, I rush to my room and quickly put on my sneakers. I accidentally got peanut butter on my shirt. But it's too late to swap it out. "Loose clothes she says, I bet this will be the easiest part of my evening, picking out loose clothes. How did I let her talk me into this?" I head back into the living room and my grandpa stops me in my tracks with a loud "HEY!"

I was hoping to sneak past without having to answer a lot of questions, I guess that's what I get for hoping. "What's up grandpa?" I ask as he reaches for me and pulls me in between him and Nana.

"I just want to know what you are up to. You have that determined look in your eyes and I know that look. So, What's up?" My grandpa asks me.

"Well, I am working on a new mystery with my friend Niko, who will be here any minute by the way. Niko also wants to show me how to defend myself. I told her that I can almost run faster than all the bullies in this neighborhood, but she insists", I say to my grandpa who just looks over at Nana with raised eyebrows. Nana only shakes her head and shrugs.

"Ok", grandpa says. "Who is Niko and how long have you two been friends?"

"Niko is a new student and we've kind of been friends since she showed up in the cafeteria", I say as I scoot forward in my attempt to slip away from the interrogation.

Luckily, the doorbell rings, and I leap up and rush to the front door. When I open the door, I find Niko smiling widely and holding what I assume is some sort of martial art practice gear.

Without saying a word, I motion for her to come inside. Grandpa and Nana come over and instead of me hoping for a quick escape to the backyard, I now have to introduce Niko to grandpa.

Grandpa comes over and does a quick bow to Niko and says something in a language other than English, Niko does a quick bow and says the same thing back. Niko and grandpa then start gibbering back and forth in 'not English' until I can't take it anymore.

"I guess there is no need for introductions now so if you're through gibbering with grandpa, we can go out back and get started", I tell Niko as I reach for the martial arts gear Niko had placed on the floor when she began talking with grandpa.

Grandpa just laughs and tells Niko, "Ok, let's go outside and find out how bad and sad this actually is."

Myself, Niko, and my grandpa all file outside with grandpa taking a seat in one of the blue cushioned chairs that faces the swimming pool.

"Alright Niko, what's first?" I ask her as we make our way to a smooth patch of grass in the backyard.

"First, Let's stretch our muscles out, so we don't accidentally pull something before we even get started", Niki says as she bends over to touch her toes.

"Well," I say as I cross my arms over my chest, "Since I don't have any muscles, I don't have to worry about pulling one. So, let's just move on."

Niko looks up at me from her bent-over position and then straightens up and grabs my right arm just below the elbow. Pain immediately shoots up my arm reminding me of the time when I was hit in the arm with a baseball. No, I wasn't playing baseball and I wasn't playing catch, but most importantly I was not paying attention. Tommy Blackwell threw a baseball at me but didn't yell for me to catch the ball until it was about 5 feet away. When he hollered at me, I turned just in time for the baseball to strike me right on the arm. I thought I was dying.

"Ow", I tell her. "What did you do that for?"

"Because you are being a goober. And that pain you felt is the nerves in your muscle that you do have. Now, let's stretch." Niko goes back to touching her toes. I look over at my grandpa and of course, he has a big grin on his face. "Ugh, why did I agree to this", I whisper under my breath.

I lean over and try to touch my toes. "Wow, I never realized my toes were so far down", I say as I strain to reach.

"Just try to touch your toes without bending your knees", Niko tells me without looking up.

"I was only thinking about it, I wasn't going to bend my knees." Wait a minute, how did Niko know what I was thinking?

After what seemed like forever and a day, Niko raises back up and says, "Ok, let's get started, Stuart."

"Now", Niko starts, "because this won't be anything like a regular lesson, we are going to forego a lot of the normal routines and katas. I believe we should get right to teaching you how to defend yourself", Niko says as she turns to face me.

"Can't we stop for a while, we've been at it for like an hour now, don't you think it's about time for a break?" I moan as I start to sit down on the grass.

"Don't you dare sit", Niko yelps at me. "We've only been outside for a few minutes".

"Argh, ok. What do you want me to do first?" I say as I take a deep breath.

"Great, the first thing I want you to do is to make a fist and strike me in the chest", Niko tells me with a sinister-looking smile on her face.

"You want me to do what? Hit you! And then you wad me up and throw me into a heap like you did Tommy Blackwell, I think not", I say crossing my arms over my chest.

"Yes, hit me, right in the chest. I promise I am not going to hurt you", Niko says, still smiling.

Against my better judgment, I pull back and take a swing at the pad Niko holds in front of her. Niko simply moves to the side, and I keep going forward until I fall on the ground a few feet behind her.

"Here, you hold the bag, and I will show you how I want you to strike, Ok?" Niko says as I pull myself from the ground.

I take the bag and hold it in front of me like she instructed and close my eyes and wait for the attack.

"Stuart, open your eyes silly. How can you see me with your eyes closed?"

I open my eyes and give Niko a sly smile, "Sorry, just a force of habit when someone is about to hit me." After a few demonstrations, Niko takes the striking bag from me and says, "Ok, your turn Rocky."

I start hitting the bag, slowly at first, and then harder and faster as my confidence grows. "This is kind of fun", I say as I hit the bag for the hundredth time. "Except my arms are getting tired."

"Ok", Niko says as she puts the bag on the ground. "Go get something to drink before you pass out on me."

I rush to the kitchen and slide into the pantry, barely stopping before crashing into the wall. I rush back to the refrigerator and grab two juice boxes and head back outside.

When I get outside, I see my grandpa and Niko going at it like two ninjas. I stare with my mouth hanging open. I haven't ever seen anything like what they were doing except on video games. Both were smiling like crazy and eventually, Niko puts my grandpa on the ground.

"That was awesome", I tell them as I walk over and give Niko a juice box.

"Yep, I hadn't had that much fun in a very long time", grandpa says as he pulls himself from the ground.

"What discipline are you Niko, I recognize some of your moves, but I am puzzled about a lot of the other", grandpa says as he does a quick bow to Niko.

"I bet you are confused about that sir. Because of my parents' work and having to move all over the world, I have been trained in aikido, ninjutsu, wushu, and krav maga" I hear Niko say as she does a quick bow back.

"Yes, I recognize the wushu and the aikido, those are two of my disciplines. The others I haven't sparred against yet", grandpa says, going into a deep stretch of some sort.

"Ok" I blurt out, "this is educational, but I am the one that needs instruction, remember".

I wished I would have just kept my mouth shut because the next hour was spent with Niko throwing me to the ground or me trying to throw her to the ground.

"You are hopeless", Niko finally says as she turns and walks over to where my grandpa is sitting next to the swimming pool.

"Rome wasn't built in a day", I yell back at her as I just lay on the ground, trying to catch my breath.

INVESTIGATION LOG

DATE: _______________ TIME: _______________

LOCATION: ____

INCIDENT DETAILS: ____

____

____

____

____

____

____

WITNESS STATEMENT: ____

____

____

____

____

NAMES LIST

VICTIM: (1)____

(2)____

WITNESS: (1)____

(2)____

SUSPECT: (1)____

(2)____

CHAPTER 9

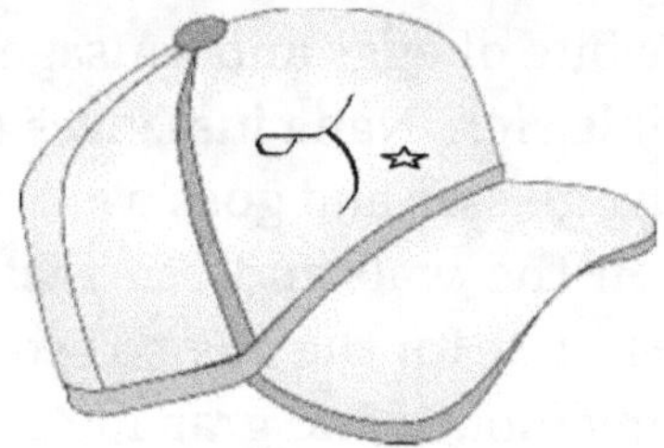

Is that what I think it is?

I wake up and attempt to roll out of bed, I mean this literally because I can hardly move my body. Niko and I have been training every evening after school for the past two weeks. Even my grandpa jumps in and trains with us sometimes. Last night's training was brutal because grandpa wanted to test me on all that I have learned so far. Every muscle and bone in my body is screaming at me.

I hear Nana from the living room telling me I have to get a shower because I took a pass on taking one last night. *Great, the only problem I have with Nana's demand is how am I supposed to get to the shower when I don't believe my legs even work anymore.*

After a long few minutes and a lot of listening to Nana yelling for me to hurry up, I am standing under the hot water, and to my surprise, I feel better now, except that I am hungrier than I have ever been in my life. The thought of something to eat has me rushing out of the shower and hurrying to get my clothes on.

My muscles now are only semi-screaming at me and not near as loud as my stomach. I make a dash for the kitchen and take a seat just as Nana is putting a plate of eggs and sausage patties down on the table in front of me. I waste no time at all as I start digging in and I am already halfway through eating my food by the time Nana places a tall glass of chocolate milk next to my plate.

I hurriedly take a big swallow of my chocolate milk to help wash down the extra-large bite of eggs and sausage I had in my mouth and give a large audible sigh. Nana just gives me one of her looks over the top of reading glasses and goes back to her phone screen.

I look at the clock on the wall and see that I only have a few minutes before I will be late for the bus, so I stuff what is left of the eggs and sausage in my mouth and grab my chocolate milk before running back to my bedroom, I mean my office.

I grab my backpack and do a quick glance to make sure I have everything, then quickly run into the bathroom, and brush my teeth so Nana won't send me back in. Then as quickly as possible, I make my way to the patio door without causing a scene.

"Bye Nana", I say as I hurry out the door without waiting for an answer.

I open the back gate to our privacy fence and poke my head out to make sure the coast is clear and see Niko standing over something on the ground. It's been a while since any items have been left and Niko and I were about to close the case. I rush over and to see what she is looking at. I look down and see a blue and red baseball cap. A very recognizable blue and red baseball cap. I would know this baseball cap anywhere, even with my eyes closed because I have seen it with my eyes closed, in my nightmares.

"This is Tommy Blackwell's baseball cap", I whisper to Niko, ever so quietly, so as not to disturb the air enough where Tommy might hear me somehow.

"Are you sure?" Niko asks me as she bends down and picks up the baseball cap.

"Absolutely cross my heart and hope that I won't now die. I can't tell you how many times I have been up close and personal with Tommy Blackwell while he was wearing that very baseball cap on his much too big head. Look on the back of the cap and I bet you will find his initials 'TB'. I know they are there because whenever I would start to tell Tommy all the reasons why he shouldn't clobber me, he would turn his head around and point to the initials and say, 'You know what TB means? It means Too Bad.' And then he would clobber me before I could say something smart-aleck back to him because you and I both know that a statement like that deserves some type of dig."

"I agree", Niko says as she takes the baseball cap and puts it in my backpack.

"What are you doing, are you trying to get me clobbered?", I yell as I quickly try and pull the backpack from my shoulders.

"You'll be fine, come on, I hear the bus coming", she says as she turns and rushes toward the game camera we still have posted at the fence and pulls the memory card out. Niko and I start walking towards the bus stop when Niko says to me, "Later today during class, I will check the memory card to see if we captured anyone on the camera." I just nod my head, I can't really focus on anything but the baseball cap in my backpack, and of course my impending doom.

We make our way onto the school bus when it stops and as we take our seat, it feels like everyone is staring at me. It's almost as if they all know I have Tommy Blackwell's baseball cap in my backpack, and they can't wait to expose me to Tommy when he gets on the bus. I feel the sudden urge to crawl back under the rear bus seat where I am comfortable and safe.

I look over and see Niko looking at me strangely. "What?", I ask her.

"You look like you are about to pass out and you appear to be sweating. Is there something wrong?", she asks as she pulls a tissue from her backpack.

Niko hands me the tissue and I wipe my forehead and I just give her my crazy person look.

"There is nothing for you to be concerned about Stuart. Also, let me do all the talking when we give Tommy his baseball cap back" Niko says and ever so calmly, folds her hands in her lap.

"I knew I should have put a clause in our partnership agreement that stated what would happen should one of us become a crazy person", I mumble out loud as I lay my head on my backpack.

I didn't have to be told when the bus was at the stop where Tommy and his cronies got on. Everyone on the bus, as always, suddenly becomes engrossed in their phones or a stain on the floor, anything to not bring attention to themselves as Tommy and his gang rumble onto the bus and make their way to their seats.

I am squirming in my seat, nervous about what Niko might be planning. She might be a miniature ninja but I'm anything but. In fact, I am probably what one would be if there was something you could classify as the exact opposite of a ninja, like maybe an anti-ninja, or ninja zero. Yes, that's what I am, ninja zero. Same height and build with none of the moves.

Dread hangs onto me like a scared cat. Which is basically what I have turned into. Niko is as calm as a frozen lake. And all too soon the bus comes to a stop in front of the school. Niko grabs me by the arm and drags me off the school bus to my impending doom.

"So, this is where it all ends for super-sleuth Stuart, the world's greatest detective mind, pummeled to death in the school cafeteria, probably ending up as tomorrow's meatloaf", I mumble quietly, and Niko gives me a puzzling look.

"No one is getting pummeled today silly", Niko tells me as we finally make it to the lockers. "We do have to come up with a foolproof plan with contingencies just in case the plan backfires though."

"So, you are still planning on telling Tommy we have his stuff, just not today, is that what you are telling me?" I ask her as I slowly sit down on the floor.

"Yes, to both of your questions. I am not crazy you know; I might be able to handle Tommy one on one, but I am no match for him and the rest of his gang all at once. So, we have to figure out a way to return his property to him without him turning on us." Niko says as she grabs her books from the locker.

"Come on Stuart, let's go to class. We can't afford to rush our plan and possibly make a mistake. That could be unfavorable to us both. Let's make sure we 'dot our I's and cross our T's", Niko says as she begins to walk off.

"I say we grab a large black plastic garbage bag and put all that useless garbage that was left on my lawn inside the garbage bag, and then take said garbage bag to some faraway dumpster and mark the case as closed so we can move on to the next case. One that doesn't involve Tommy Blackwell", I say as I catch up to her.

"You know that is not a proper way to close out a case, we need to return all of the "stolen" property to its rightful owner", Niko tells me as we sit down in our first class.

"I'm the owner now, it's abandoned property and I now claim it as my own," I say to Niko. "So, since I am the owner, I say we dig a hole and bury it somewhere."

"Stuart", Niko says while shaking her head, "sometimes you just crack me up."

"Yeah, well, I seem to do that to a lot of people", I tell her as I lay my head down on my desk.

I heard our preacher say one Sunday that one day is like a thousand years to God. Well, I am no deity, but I understand how that feels. I have been waiting on the final bell to ring to officially end the longest day of my life for what seems like an eternity. And to make matters worse, Niko says she still doesn't have a plan to return Tommy's property without us both getting clobbered to bits.

Finally, I hear the wonderful sound of the final bell that lets the students know it is time to go home.

Neither of us says hardly a word to each other on the school bus ride home, and by the time we get off the school bus, my mind is made up. I am grabbing some clothes and defecting to Canada.

Niko stops on the sidewalk as we were walking towards our respective homes and so naturally, I stop also. Niko turns to face me with a smile on her face and says, "I think I have a plan. Of course, I will need to write it out when I get home to ensure there are no mistakes or flaws, but I believe it will work."

Niko turns and starts walking again as I just stand there with my eyes bugging out and my mouth hanging open. "Hey", I shout to Niko, but she simply continues to walk on, "So you're just going to leave me hanging? You're not going to tell me about your master plan that's supposed to keep me from getting pulverized into hamburger meat?"

Niko waved her hand up in the air and said something to me, but she was too far away now for me to hear clearly. "Okay then", I say as I start walking to my house, "I suppose I need to pack for cold weather, I believe Canada is pretty much iced over this time of the year."

INVESTIGATION LOG

DATE: _______________ TIME: _______________

LOCATION: ____

INCIDENT DETAILS: ____

____

____

____

____

____

____

WITNESS STATEMENT: ____

____

____

____

____

NAMES LIST

VICTIM: (1)____

(2)____

WITNESS: (1)____

(2)____

SUSPECT: (1)____

(2)____

CHAPTER 10

The Plan, The Plan!

After a peanut butter fold-over and a juice box, I felt a little less stressed. I still have Canada as a workable option, that is if I can somehow get my passport from my dad's office safe.

I grab my smart tablet from its charger and flop down on my bed. Nothing calms a person down like a good game of Call of Duty. I am about midways into wiping out a band of terrorists when a message pops up on my tablet.

"STUART, I BELIEVE I HAVE ALL THE BUGS WORKED OUT."

I read the message and I am shocked and confused. First, I am shocked because I received a message on my tablet, no one has ever messaged me before. Two, I am confused because I don't know anything about bugs and how they do their workout. I didn't even know bugs worked out.

I type a reply to the message, "WHO IS THIS?"

"THIS IS NIKO SILLY", the message on my screen says.

"OH", I send back. "NIKO, HOW DID YOU SEND ME A MESSAGE? AND NIKO, WHY ARE YOU PLAYING WITH BUGS?"

"WHAT?" Niko replies. 'NEVER MIND, CAN YOU COME OVER?"

"YEAH MAYBE, ARE YOU THROUGH WORKING OUT, I DON'T HAVE THE ENERGY TO WORK OUT TODAY?" I message back to Niko.

"DUDE!", Niko responds. "JUST COME OVER."

I grab my tack-pack and make my way to the patio door. I wave at my nana and tell her I am heading over to Niko's for a little while. Nana waves back and tells me to be back before suppertime. Well, I am not agreeing to that without knowing what is on the menu, plus I may be halfway to Canada by then.

Not wanting to get caught on the sidewalk alone by Tommy or one of his goons, I semi-race to Niko's house and make it there in what I believe to be record time.

Niko meets me at the door with a juice box which is perfect since I ran all the way over. I pull the little straw off the side of the box and shove it into the top and take a long hard sip. "Ah! that hits the spot", I say as Niko turns and motions for me to follow.

When we get to her bedroom, she motions for me to sit in a chair that she has facing towards a whiteboard. I sit and stare at the whiteboard suspiciously, seeing that there are multiple diagrams and notes listed under each one. Then over to the side of the board is a list numbered 1 through 10.

"Are we planning a coup?" I ask her as I take another draw from my juice box.

"I am delighted to hear that you even know what that word means, it gives me hope in this investigative adventure", Niko tells me as she walks over to the whiteboard.

"This padawan is our plan. So, pay attention and take notes and feel free to ask questions as we go along", Niko starts. "Ok, first on the agenda, let's compile all the evidence, I'm sorry, let me correct myself, it is no longer evidence but recovered property. First, let's compile all the recovered property into one box so it will be easier to carry. The box will have Tommy's name on it in big bold letters. Then, step two we will…, what is it, Stuart?" Niko says as she finally sees my hands waving in the air.

"One question", I say as I put my hand back down, "Wouldn't it be easier to bury the stuff separately, digging several small holes will be easier than trying to bury them all at once?"

"We are not going to bury the property, Stuart", Niko says as she turns and points towards the whiteboard again. "As I was saying, step two we will…for Pete's sake Stuart now what?" Niko says as she sees my hand in the air waving again.

"Won't a box large enough to put all the recovered property in be difficult to burn without someone noticing?" I ask Niko.

"Stuart, we are not going to burn, bury or destroy the property in any way, form or fashion, we are going to return all of the property to its rightful owner," Niko says rather loudly.

"Now", Niko starts again, "Step Two", Niko pauses and looks at me for a moment, "We carry the box containing all the property over to our neighborhood park."

"Wow, that's brilliant Niko. We just drop all his property off in the park in the box with his name on it, run like crazy, and let someone else explain to Tommy why his belongings are in the park", I exclaim as I fist pump in the air a few times.

"Well, you are half right Stewart", Niko says. "We are going to place the box with his belongings in the park, but not just in the park, on the pitcher's mound at the ball field area. Then, after we make a clean exit and are safely back at home, I am going to anonymously text Tommy Blackwell to tell him that all his lost items are in a box at the park on the pitcher's mound", Niko tells me excitedly.

"I love the plan Niko; I only have one question. How are we going to get the box to the park.? The box is not heavy, at least for me of course, but it is rather bulky, and it will be hard to carry from here to the park", I tell Niko, disappointment in my tone.

"Not to worry Stuart, if you look at the diagram on the board under item number three, you will find that I have accounted for the difficulty in transporting the large carton", Niko says in a factual tone, then continues, "I have secured the use of my mom's garden wagon for our excursion to the park".

"Wow Niko, I guess you did think of everything. Well, what do you say, are you ready to put this fine plan of yours in motion?" I ask her as I hurriedly finish my juice box.

"Absolutely", Niko answers back. Niko grabs her tack-pack as we both turn to leave her bedroom and head outside. We leave the patio door into her backyard. I follow Niko around to the side of her house and over to a small garden shed from which Niko pulls a small green garden wagon from inside.

We leave Niko's yard through the side gate fence and begin a normal pace trek back to my house where I have all of Tommy's recovered items sealed in plastic bags.

We arrive at my house and go inside, leaving the wagon outside by the patio door.

Once in my office/bedroom, I begin retrieving Tommy's property I had sealed in bags from my file cabinet/dresser and commence placing them on my bed.

Niko breaks the seal on the first item and a nasty odor fills the room. "Wow, maybe I should have left that one sealed up. This is rank", Niko says as she chunks the sneaker back on the bed.

"No way", I tell her. "If Tommy finds his shoe all sealed up in a bag with the word 'EVIDENCE' written on it, he will immediately know it was me who put it there."

"Yeah, you are probably right", Niko replies. "But what if we mark through the word 'EVIDENCE' and write 'SMELL AFTER OPENING'. He would pass out after sucking in the air from the bag and probably wake up with brain damage and wouldn't remember anything", Niko says and starts laughing hysterically.

I join in and we both fall on the bed laughing, that is until we get another whiff of the sneaker. That of course brings on a few gags, which in turn causes us to start laughing again.

After we get all the property out of the plastic bags and stack them in a pile, I let out a loud sigh. "Ok", I say to Niko, "Now that we have all the property ready to go, all we need is a box. Do you have a box at your house Niko?"

"No, I don't have a box, I thought you would have a box", Niko replies as she turns and flops on the bed beside Tommy's stuff.

"Aw man, I don't have a box. What are we going to do now?" I grumble as I flop down on the bed beside Niko.

"Wait a minute, let me go ask Nana if she knows where a box is. Hold on I will be right back", I tell Niko as I jump up from the bed and head towards the hallway.

I look through the house and then open the back patio door where I find my Nana, sitting in her favorite chair playing on her phone.

"Hey Nana", I say as I walk outside and over to where she is sitting. "I need a box to put some stuff in, do you have a box?"

"How big of a box?" Nana replies, sitting her phone in her lap.

"Oh, about this big", I say as I hold my hand apart from each other. "And about this tall".

"Nope, I don't have one", Nana says as she picks her phone back up.

"It doesn't have to be that exact size of a box, really any box will do", I tell Nana.

"Nope, still don't have one", Nana tells me without looking up from her phone.

"Why would you ask me how big of a box I needed if you don't have one?" I ask, now feeling a little frustrated.

"Oh, I was just curious that's all", Nana says as she looks up from her phone and smiles at me. "Why don't you just put whatever it is that you had planned on putting in the box, into a plastic garbage bag? Unless of course it's too fragile and may break."

"Actually Nana, that is genius. Thanks", I tell her as I turn and run back inside.

I hurry to the pantry where I know there are several different sizes of plastic garbage bags. I quickly grab one of the large black plastic garbage bags from the carton, then I open it up by shaking it a few times. "Perfect", I say as I scurry back to my office.

As I walk into my room, I find Niko sitting in the same position on my bed, going through my smart tablet as if she owned it. "You have quite a lot of pictures stored on your tablet Stuart; I do hope you are backing them up if they are case-related".

I give Niko my best eye roll. "There is a slight change of plans Niko. I couldn't find a box, so I grabbed a plastic garbage bag, we'll just put all of Tommy's belongings in it instead", I say as I'm shaking the plastic bag again, attempting to open the bag as large as possible.

"That's more suitable for all this junk than a nice box anyway. Just print out Tommy's name and address on a sheet of paper and we will tape it to the bag when we get to the park", Niko says as she jumps up from the bed.

I hand Niko the bag, "Ok, you start stuffing, and I will start printing".

"We're headed to the park Nana", I yell as we exit through the patio door. I hear Nana tell me to be back in time for supper as I close the door. I wouldn't dream of missing whatever green gooey concoction she has invented for dinner this evening. Nana has been on a health kick ever since grandpa came back home. Personally, I can live off peanut butter sandwiches.

Niko and I start walking towards the fence gate and out of habit for my wellbeing, I open the gate only a little and poke my head out and have a look around. Seeing no one around in either direction, I open the gate fully and walk out onto the sidewalk as if I own it.

"You are seriously paranoid my friend", Niko tells me as she follows me onto the sidewalk.

"Years of self-preservation is all", I answer her back with a grin on my face. For some reason I feel almost giddy, maybe it is because I will finally be getting rid of all of Tommy Blackwell's junk, and I can close this case. Yeah, I'm sure that's what has me bouncing with excitement, this stuff has made me uneasy ever since I found out who it all belonged to.

I have the plastic garbage slung over my shoulder like a hobo as we head directly to the neighborhood park. There was no need to bring the wheelbarrow since we did not put the items in a box. This worked out better in my professional opinion.

The neighborhood park is mostly deserted because it is getting near to most people's dinner time. There are a few young children on the sliding board and climbing station along with their mothers standing close by, but other than those few, the park is clear.

Niko and I stroll across the park to where the picnic tables are located, neither of us talking, I guess we are both lost in our thoughts. We walk over to one of the tables in the middle of the picnic area and I plop the bag down on the tabletop. "Whew", I say as I let out a breath of air. "That is starting to get heavy."

"Yeah, I probably should have carried for you", Niko says with a grin.

"Yeah, you're hilarious", I say as I pull the folded piece of paper with Tommy's name written on it from my pocket. "Why don't we just leave it here on the table, it is as good of a place as any, and the ball field is still a long walk from here", I say as I quickly unfold the paper and lay it flat up against the side of the plastic garbage bag. Being careful not to tear the paper, I smooth out all the wrinkles and then hold my hands out for the roll of tape I know that Niko has in her hands.

"Just hold the paper steady", she tells me. "I will tape it to the bag. I've seen your taping abilities in art class at school. The chances of you taping yourself to the bag are really high".

"Yeah? Well, I guess since you've seen how a real detective solves a case, you've decided it would be in your best interest to become a comedian now". I tell Niko as I move my hands away from where she is taping the paper to the plastic garbage bag.

"Who's being the comedian now?" Niko says as she tapes the last corner of the paper to the garbage bag.

We both step back and admire our handiwork when I hear from behind us, "Well, well, well. What do we have here boys?"

I slowly turn around and see Tommy Blackwell and his three cronies.

Of all the rotten luck and bad timing that has transpired in my lifetime, I think this probably ranks just below Nana sitting on my smart tablet and breaking the screen.

"What's that sitting on the table behind you? Are you two on a little picnic together?" Tommy says and all his buddies start laughing. "I don't know about you guys, but I'm starving."

Tommy and his gang start towards the picnic table and Niko, and I slowly try and move in the opposite direction. Niko leans over and whispers "Can you outrun these guys?"

I Look over at Niko and attempt my best impersonation of her eye roll.

"Well, I guess that's a no then", she whispers again. "I'm mostly sure that I can. And I suppose the next few moments will define our friendship."

"Save yourself and go", I whisper back. "I promise there won't be any hard feelings. I've been in these situations numerous times. This is not my first time having to deal with bullies and it won't be my last, that is if I survive of course."

I could see Niko weighing her options over and looking around for the easiest exit when I heard Tommy shout, and I knew then that the time to escape had now passed. Niko had a chance while they were all focused on the garbage bag, thinking they had a free lunch. But now, all their attention was on me and Niko.

"Hey nerds", Tommy yells, "Why is my name and address taped to your lunch?"

I turn and face Tommy's direction and watch his eyes grow large and his face turns red as he opens the garbage bag and looks inside.

"It's not what it looks like Tommy", I tell him, knowing all the while I am wasting my time trying to explain, but nevertheless, I keep going. "We are just trying to return your stuff; we didn't take it."

"Really", Tommy starts, "Is that why you are dropping it here in the middle of the park instead of knocking on my door? It doesn't look like you are trying to return it, it looks like you are leaving it up for grabs for whoever comes by."

"Well, when you put it that way, our actions do seem suspicious." I say to Tommy, "But trust me, all we wanted to do was make sure all your items made it back to you." *And for you not to have any idea that we had anything to do with it,* I think to myself.

 "Sure, sure, that's all you wanted," Tommy says as he and his goons start walking toward me and Niko. "I'm going to bust you up nerd-boy, and your girlfriend will be too busy with my pals to help you this time."

I see Niko get into her fighting stance beside me, I would do the same, but I don't think it would do any good. My body had a different opinion because as Tommy came up in front of me, I noticed I had shifted my feet and weight just like Niko had taught me.

I know from experience that as soon as Tommy gets close enough to punch, he will. And just as expected, he throws a wild punch at my head. I guess all that training with Niko taught me something because I duck under his punch with ease. I know there is another punch coming from his other hand and I duck away from it easily also.

I am not a violent person, so I don't try to hit Tommy back, and so far, he hasn't hurt me. And I do believe that me grinning at Tommy is not helping his anger issues, but I can't help myself. For the first time in my life, I have kept myself from being pummeled by a bully.

Tommy reaches and grabs me by the shirt and pulls me to him, "You think you are some kind of tough guy now nerd-boy", Tommy says as he draws back to hit me again.

Thankfully, Niko and I practiced this same scenario until I could do it in my sleep. The old grabbing the nerd by the shirt ploy and beating him senseless scenario. I quickly grab Tommy's hand that he is holding my shirt with and twist it around towards his elbow and shove him away.

I quickly glance over at Niko and observe that one of Tommy's goons is on the ground rubbing his knee and another goon is on his knees with both hands covering his private parts and a look of pain on his face.

I turn back to Tommy, and I can see that anger is not the word to describe what his face is expressing. I believe the proper term would be rage and not anger. And if it were physically possible, there would be steam coming from his ears like a cartoon.

Well, unless Tommy grabs me by the shirt again, I am out of moves that will keep me from being pummeled. As Tommy steps back in front of me, I can only guess the only thing going on in his tiny little brain is where to hit me first.

With his mind made up, Tommy pulls back with his right fist to punch, and I close my eyes to wait for my impending doom. But a terrifying low growl from behind me causes Tommy to freeze in his tracks. Tommy looks behind me and starts to say, "What the", but he is cut off by another terrifying growl, and this time there is more than one creature growling.

No one is moving at this point; Tommy still has his fist pulled back but is not moving a muscle. I risk a peek at Niko and see that she and the goons are looking behind me with terror written on their faces.

I don't know whether to be glad or scared now. On the one hand, I am not getting pummeled by Tommy, but on the other hand, I might be about to get eaten by a bear.

Tommy looks over at his friends and motions with his head to back away. In unison, they all begin to slowly back away from me and Niko. The growling is getting louder now, and Niko says, "Don't move Stuart, and please don't turn around."

Well crap, now I have to turn around.

Just as I start to slowly turn around, Tommy makes it to the picnic table and grabs his bag of junk. "Hey nerds, unless you two become a permanent chew toy, this isn't over."

Tommy and his buddies all laugh as they turn and start running towards the park exit. I feel something brush against my leg as two brown blurs speed past and streak towards Tommy and his crew.

I watch as the two growling creatures begin to close the distance to within mere yards of Tommy. I can't see their faces, but I can hear their screams as they all scatter in different directions.

The two animals halt and sit on their haunches.

I am torn between two emotions, scared, and confused. I am confused because I have no idea what has just happened, and I am scared because the two muscle-bound fur-covered creatures are trotting their way back to me and Niko.

As the two animals approach, I hear Niko exclaim "Oh, now I understand, well some of it anyway."

I look over at her like she's lost her mind but then I catch movement out of the corner of my eye.

I look back and find that the two fur-covered creatures are in fact big dogs. Very big dogs. As they get closer to me, they both start doing some sort of wiggling dance with their whole bodies.

"Wait a minute", I say as I stare at the two dogs. "I know these two. I recognize the little dance that they're doing, it's called the jellybean or something like that."

"Well then, please explain to me how you know these two giant dogs. I believe that the answer to our case riddle lies in how you came to know these two dogs", Niko says as she kneels down and calls the dogs over.

I sit down on the ground beside Niko and we both start petting each of the dogs, as best as we can anyway, the two dogs are doing their little dance so hard and fast it is hard to keep up with them long enough to pet.

"It all started a couple of months ago", I begin. "Dogs from our neighborhood began to go missing. It started with just one, then another, and then another. By the third dog, I was already on the case. It took me a couple of weeks, but I tracked the bad guy down and rescued the dogs from their captor."

"So, were these dogs victims of the dog-napper?" Niko asks.

"Only one, this one here with the white on her nose. Her name is Belle, her sister's name is Anna. They are called Boxers", I say as I try in vain to hold Belle in one place to pet her.

"Anna, Belle, seriously, that's their names? And they are called Boxers? Do they box?", Niko asks.

"Ha, not that I am aware of, but I do know that their breed has been around for a long time and that during one of the World Wars, the Boxer was used to deliver messages", I tell Niko.

"Well, I can tell you that Belle is the culprit that has been dropping off the little presents in your yard. The game camera caught her with Tommy's hat in between her teeth. I wasn't sure what was going on at the time, but now I understand. Remember I told you I would look at the memory card while I was in class? Well, I did, and I saw Belle in the picture. Of course, I didn't know it was Belle then, but now that I know the whole story, it all makes sense" Niko tells me as she stands up.

"At least it makes sense to you, I still don't understand it", I tell

Niko.

Niko grabs my hand and helps me to my feet and says, "Come on, let head back home and I will tell you my theory as we walk.

Niko and I brush off the leaves stuck to our clothes and start walking to the park exit.

"Ok, here is my theory", Niko starts. "I believe that Belle has formed some sort of a bond with you because of you rescuing her. And all those so-called gifts she has been bringing to you are tokens of appreciation. I am not sure if she knows that you and Tommy are mortal enemies, but if she does, that would make my theory even cooler."

"I got to say, I like your theory better than mine. I was thinking that Belle and her sister Anna were taking up a life of crime. And since I am the neighborhood detective, they were planning on framing me with all the thefts to get rid of me", I say as I nervously check my surroundings for Tommy and his gang.

"Wow, you have some kind of imagination going on in that brain of yours", Niko says with a laugh.

"Ha", I start, "You have no idea what all goes on inside this head of mine."

"Nope, and I am sure I don't want to know either", Niko replies. "Let's get home and finish the paperwork on this case and close it out"

"By the way, what was that little silent exchange you had with your mom when we first met?" I ask Niko.

"Oh, you saw that did you, Mr. Detective Extraordinaire? Well, I might as well clue you in now…girls have secrets. Always have and always will", Niko tells me with a grin on her face. "I'm ready for another case, how about you?"

"Absolutely", I say. "There is this strange house I found on a dead-end street, the house looks abandoned but as I was walking past it one afternoon, I thought I saw someone in the window. I have been wanting to investigate it but haven't had the opportunity yet." *And I am too scared to go back to that creepy old place by myself.*

"Sounds like a plan, partner", Niko says as we head down the street, the two Boxers at our heels. I feel safe with those two with us, I wonder if Mrs. Johnston, the dogs' owner, would let me borrow them whenever I need to walk through the neighborhood. I know, I could tell her that I have started a dog walking business and even get her to pay me for walking her dogs.

I really am a genius.

The End, that is until my next case.